NORTH OF MULHOLLAND

Essays from the
San Fernando Valley Business Journal

Martin M. Cooper

authorHOUSE®

AuthorHouse™
1663 Liberty Drive
Bloomington, IN 47403
www.authorhouse.com
Phone: 1-800-839-8640

© 2010 Martin M. Cooper. All rights reserved.

No part of this book may be reproduced, stored in a retrieval system, or transmitted by any means without the written permission of the author.

First published by AuthorHouse 3/19/2010

ISBN: 978-1-4490-8213-0 (e)
ISBN: 978-1-4490-8212-3 (sc)
ISBN: 978-1-4490-8211-6 (hc)

Library of Congress Control Number: 2010901325

Printed in the United States of America
Bloomington, Indiana

This book is printed on acid-free paper.

To Barbara

My wife and biggest supporter

Acknowledgements

Reviewing nearly five years of essays in preparing *North of Mulholland* for publication was not the simple task I had imagined it would be. Luckily, I have a first-rate support mechanism, and this is an appropriate arena in which to express my appreciation for their assistance:

The entire staff of the *San Fernando Valley Business Journal*, for their unwavering support of my writings. Particular thanks to Publisher Pegi Matsuda and Editor Jason Schaff, who has generally been referred to throughout as Ye Olde Editor, despite his youth.

Stewart Deats of Deats Design, who contributed the cover concept and design, with a photograph that perfectly matches the book title.

Jan Sobel, my very good friend for many years, who copyread the book and offered numerous suggestions, almost all of them excellent.

Terry Stevens, my able assistant, who put up with my wildest of ideas without rolling her eyes heavenward and cheerfully ignored the fact that I spent hours on this book that could have been invested more gainfully.

Phyllis Townsend, my sister, who endures my teasing about living in Visalia but good-naturedly read the manuscript.

Bill Carpenter of the Los Angeles Valley College Historical Museum, for providing photographs and caption information.

The staff of the Oviatt Library of California State University, Northridge, for some of the historic photographs.

And all the people of the San Fernando Valley, without whom this book would not be possible.

Contents

Acknowledgements	vii
Introduction	xiii

2005
The Valley: A City in All but Name	1
When Too Many Valley Businesses Have Died …	5
No Beauty Contest Winners in the Valley	9
Valley Residents, Firms Returning Favor	14
City Council Needs to Rethink Its Priorities	18
Bullish on the Valley, but Russia Is a Bear	22
Trying to Get a Read on News Rack Mess	26
Be Resolute in Helping Valley Business	30

2006
Lonely at the Top But Often Lucrative	34
Bookworm's Homage to the Printed Word	39
School's Out on the Mayor's Plan for LAUSD	43
Time to Develop a Business Attraction Program	47
Ten Years – And a Lot Hasn't Changed	52
A Very Real Truth – Inconvenient or Not	56
Mel and Andy: Two Birdbrains of a Feather	60
A Real Bull Story with a Moral for Business	64
Marketing Philanthropy: Getting by Giving	67
We Get *What* in Return for Four More Years?	71

Now We'll be Doing it by the Numbers 75
It's What's Next That Counts in the Valley 79

2007
Labor Wins, Business Loses – Again 84
A Modest Proposal to the Successful 88
It's True: The Times They are A-Changin' 92
Valley Business: Diversity at Work 96
A Classless Society with No Class 100
There's No Sense at the Census 104
Leaving California for Nebraska? 107
Valley Fights Whites-Only Image 111
Sub-Par Thinking On Sub-Prime Loans 115
The Professor Tells it Like it Is 119
Tale of Kvelling in Canoga Park 123
Settling for Less than Utopia 127

2008
In Praise of the Type Cast Machine 132
It's Tough to Do the Right Thing 136
There Really Is a Here, Here 140
"To Serve and Protect" – Us 145
What's the Valley's Gross National Happiness? 149
Barking at the Dog Days of Summer 154
Turning the Page on the *Los Angeles Times* 158
Water – Not Oil – Will be Source of Conflict 163
Terrible Trio Takes its Toll but This Too Shall Pass 167
Ninety Years Ago this Month, but Only a Fleeting Memory 171
A November Ritual We Can Do Without 175

May I Have a Word With You?	179
A Trip to the Bookstore: Reading, Redux	184

2009

Billy: He's an Elephant WE Won't Forget	188
White Hats and Black Hats	193
America's Newspapers are Dying. So What?	197
Hail the American Song Book	203
We Americans Give Good Hate	209
No "Thriller" of a Media Event in Encino	214
I Invented the Cell Phone	219
Missed Opportunities…and Missed Pleasures	223
Showing Their Mettle with a Medal	227
What's the Valley's Next Big Thing?	231
Cause-Related Marketing Good for the Bottom Line	235
AT&T's Sales Scam: They're Phoning It In	240

I enjoy reading the *Business Journal*—even when traveling to Kuala Lumpur, Malaysia. Behind me are the tallest twin towers in the world, one of them sprouting from my head.

Introduction

Los Angeles has produced some great newspaper columnists: Jack Smith, Jim Murray, Al Martinez, Steve Lopez, and Dennis McCarthy. Ever since my adolescent days as editor of the Mark Twain Junior High School *Riverboat*, I wanted to be one of them.

But along with my plans to be a star power forward for the Lakers or bedazzle critics by writing the Great American Novel (okay, I'd have settled for a place in the top ten), it was not to be.

I moved to the Valley in 1971 and have operated my own marketing and public relations firm, Cooper Communications, Inc., here since 1982. Although our clients have come from around the world, including London, Australia, Jerusalem, and even Brunei, our focus has largely been on Los Angeles and the San Fernando Valley. At last count our Valley-based client list has topped one hundred organizations, corporations, and other business entities.

That business focus has been accompanied by significant involvement in the Valley's civic, community, and philanthropic affairs.

In that context, Jason Schaff, editor of the *San Fernando Valley Business Journal,* thought I might have something to say about where our ever-changing Valley has been, where it is, and where it may be headed.

Although my monthly essay usually focused on business trends and opinion, and commentary on current business issues, it often ventured into my eclectic interests, from antique typewriters to books and from urban architectural preservation to Winston Churchill. My penchant for relevant quotations from well-known people manifested itself at the end of each column.

In rereading these 57 commentaries I find some sadly outdated but others still current. In one or two rare instances I have even been prescient. Take Angelo Mozilo, for instance. I took him to task long before the unraveling of Countrywide Home Loans and the house-of-cards economic tumble that followed.

All of the profits from the sale of *North of Mulholland* will be donated to San Fernando philanthropies I have supported over the years.

I've had great fun writing these commentaries and even engendered a hate letter or two in reaction. If you enjoy reading them half as much as I enjoyed writing them, you'll be well ahead of the price of the book.

—Martin M. Cooper
Encino, California

The Valley: A City in All but Name

The Valley's business community owes its success, in large part, to our love of cars and our hatred of the roads on which we drive them.

The mystique of the late, lamented "Car Capital of the World" title we once claimed is long dissipated, as is the pleasure of the Sunday afternoon drive; the sneaking into the car dealership the week before the official unveiling of the new models; weekend cruising on Van Nuys Boulevard; and the thrill of decking, shaving, pinstriping, or flaming our 350-horsepower muscle cars.

Much as we loved those gas-guzzling vehicular behemoths, our inability to provide the roads to handle them doomed (or blessed) us with the imperative of creating a society we could get to without spending our lives behind the wheel.

Cheap post–World War II housing brought hundreds of thousands of ambitious young people to the Valley. But by the early '60s, the Cahuenga Pass, Old Sepulveda Boulevard (there never was a New Sepulveda Boulevard), and a few windy canyon roads, were all that was available for on-the-rise executives to get to their downtown, mid-Wilshire or Westside jobs.

How we rejoiced when, in 1962, the 405 Freeway arrived to set us free. But our own unchecked growth, resulting from inexpensive housing coupled with the thirst others had for our endless summers and the potential for movie stardom, taught us that suburbia can choke on its own traffic just as well as urban centers can. And the upstream developments from the likes of Santa Clarita, Thousand Oaks, and Lancaster didn't help.

It became increasingly challenging to get to jobs in that storied metropolis known as "over the hill." So we brought the jobs here to the Valley ... and the people who went with them.

We created restaurants in which to feed them, hospitals in which to cure them, schools in which to educate them, and retail stores to satisfy their consumerist urges. And we built office buildings along Ventura Boulevard, Warner Center, the Burbank Media Center, and others, including, to our everlasting urban design shame, the strip mall.

We realized that the necessities of business life were all to be had without venturing into that city of which we were a part, but from which we were becoming increasingly alienated.

We talked about "going into the city" for a meeting or social engagement as if we were not part of Los Angeles, but a separate entity. In fact, many here felt that they lived and worked in a separate city, in all but law.

And so, we come to the threshold question, "Are we part of Los Angeles or not?" We've all heard the canards about how the Valley would be the nation's sixth-largest city if we were a separate metropolis, how we are underrepresented in the corridors of City

Hall, that we provide the city with more in tax dollars than we receive in city services.

But are we truly ready to be a separate city? Where is our avenue of art galleries, performance centers, or art museums? Can you name just ten major philanthropists who support the Valley's growth and development? Have we really created a separate and distinct identity? Can we ever create a "downtown" of the Valley?

Our biggest companies, Boeing, Disney, and Amgen, exist to meet the needs not of the Valley and its people, but of the nation and the world.

But despite the fact that we lack many of the amenities of a large metropolis and major homegrown industries, perhaps we really *are* a separate city, with our own institutions, our own traditions, and our own future.

Maybe secession is a state of mind, a point of view. More than 50 percent of us voted to be our own municipality. Perhaps we've become a separate city (made up of many communities) simply because it became so easy to live and work here. Taxes and government tie us to Los Angeles, but perhaps we've become a separate city in our hearts and minds ... and maybe that's what matters most.

Maybe we should stop worrying about what Los Angeles is doing to us and start focusing on what we can do for ourselves. The result of too many people – and their cars – is that we've created our own de facto city. So let's get on with building it.

Let us not curse the late-but-not-lamented Caltrans diamond lanes, slides in Coldwater Canyon, or Sigalerts (named after my late friend Lloyd Sigmon, of KMPC Radio). Without them we'd still be working ... "over the hill."

∗∗∗

Our vast progress in transportation, past and future, is only a symbol of the progress that is possible by constantly striving toward new horizons in every human activity. Who can say what new horizons lie before us if we can but maintain the initiative and develop the imagination to penetrate them – new economic horizons, new horizons in the art of government, new social horizons.

—Alfred P. Sloan Jr.

When Too Many Valley Businesses Have Died ...

I find it sad when Valley businesses die.

It's like losing an old friend when familiar doors are shuttered, sometimes to open a few weeks later as something else, sometimes to fall prey to emotionless bulldozers.

I miss Du-Par's at the corner of Hayvenhurst and Petit in Encino. It opened in 1957 and closed in 1984 – a twenty-seven-year run. It was replaced by Eddie Saul's deli, featuring that irascible waitress, Sue. Today, Jerry's Famous Deli has food that is too common and prices that are too high to think of it with much affection.

I miss eating at Tracton's in Encino, Tail o' the Cock on Ventura Boulevard near Coldwater Canyon, the King's Arms in Toluca Lake, Phil Ahn's Moongate in Panorama City, Otto's Pink Pig on Van Nuys, and even Don Drysdale's Dugout on Oxnard in Van Nuys. What's now a modest Italian restaurant across from Encino Park used to be Stratton's, and before that, Encino Hardware.

I miss gawking at the outrageous outfits at Nudie's Western Wear in North Hollywood, listening to jazz at Dante's on Lankershim Boulevard, fishing for trout at Sportsman's Lodge, strolling past the booths at the

Valley Fair at Devonshire Downs, and wearing boots once a year to Richard Katz's fund-raisers at the Palomino Club.

Evolution is natural; change is inevitable.

But what isn't inevitable is the continued neglect of support for our own home-grown businesses.

I don't mean that we should all run out and see every Disney film because that studio is in Burbank, or that we must forsake every other brand of brew because Anheuser-Busch continues to sweeten the air with the odor of malt near the 405 and Roscoe Boulevard (although it's hard to resist the charms of a really good Disney animated film or those of a Bud Lite).

The large corporations can generally take care of themselves when it comes to marketing. No one can promote a film like Disney; no one can sell a beer like Budweiser. And even if we wanted to, it would be difficult to go down to the store and buy a Boeing product.

The furniture stores aren't better in Ventura, the clothing stores aren't trendier in Santa Monica, and the bookstores don't have any more volume in West Hollywood.

We bemoan having to drive "over the hill" to get to our offices or to meetings, but we don't hesitate to drive farther than we have to when it comes to shopping or entertainment.

Years ago, when my firm represented the Pasadena Playhouse, I was fascinated to learn that, next to the zip code in which the Playhouse was located, more season ticket holders came from the 91436 (Encino) zip code than any other in the entire city. We have the Autry Center, the Skirball Cultural Center, the Madrid Theatre, Concerts in the Park, and much more, but somehow we don't hesitate to seek entertainment outside the Valley.

What would happen if we all made a point of spending our money here?

If we shopped in local clothing stores, we'd look just as good as if we had shopped at the Beverly Center (maybe better)! Our restaurants are just as good as those anyplace in the region. Our doctors, dentists, lawyers, and accountants are every bit as proficient as those of Beverly Hills, Westwood, or downtown.

Why don't the nearly two dozen chambers that represent the business community of our area, the Valley Economic Alliance, or any of our other business groups urge us to spend our money here?

The advantage of such a program would not be merely jingoistic self-promotion, but would give us all the opportunity to discover the broad variety and impressive number of retail establishments that cover the Valley and serve its residents and businesses.

Focusing on circulating our money across the Valley is true economic development. It is not as glamorous as enticing another employer with 500 jobs to relocate here, but it *is* the kind of easily implemented program that will help keep our own business community healthy; Valley-based businesses will be less likely to think of migrating to either surrounding communities perceived as being more business friendly, or to other states.

We have to leave it to the politicians in City Hall and our state's capital to deal with issues such as business tax and workers' comp reform, but we can be masters of our own economic fate when it comes to deciding what businesses we will support with our own dollars.

Which brings me back to the subject of restaurants. If we all promised to eat every meal out in a restaurant north of Mulholland, I wouldn't have to be nostalgic for Valley restaurants that once were but are no longer.

***

Some people regard private enterprise as a predatory tiger to be shot. Others look on it as a cow they can milk. Not enough people see it as a healthy horse, pulling a sturdy wagon.
—Sir Winston Churchill

No Beauty Contest Winners in the Valley

The Valley is ugly.

There, I've said it and I'm glad.

It probably wasn't any great shakes when the Chumash and the San Gabrielino Native Americans were around. Lots of dry scrub and precious little water, even then.

But at least they didn't import the cypress, palms, and other vegetative interlopers that have resulted in a hodgepodge of arboreal looks. And that's not even mentioning that toxic and ubiquitous oleander, a shrub that has morphed into the San Fernando Valley National Plant.

But if we've transgressed against the natural habitat, what we've done with our buildings is the architectural equivalent of a capital crime.

Ripe as they are for ridicule and revulsion, let's not focus on the homes we've constructed, those little cracker boxes built starting in the late '40s, later replaced with the graceful California ranch style. Now that look is disappearing into mansions too big for their lots and homes whose designs are as out of place in their neighborhoods as a Bentley would be on Keyes Honda's lot.

Take a look at where we shop.

Indoor shopping is not a recent innovation. In Persia, Isfahan's Grand Bazaar dates from the tenth century. London's graceful Burlington Arcade opened in 1819. The first U.S. mall was The Arcade in Providence, Rhode Island, built in 1828. The Northridge Mall, the Galleria, The Plant, and any number of retail malls designed to separate us from our money all lack beauty, grace, and any sense of style.

Our Valley became famous (and perhaps reviled) for popularizing the strip mall, that ugly group of stucco-clad buildings set back from the street and fronted by an asphalt-covered parking lot.

Los Angeles' city planners decided that the best way to develop the Valley was to lay out a grid of major thoroughfares – Ventura, Van Nuys, Roscoe, Sherman Way, and so on – and build all the retail and office space along them. No thought was given to creating villages where people could walk to school and to stores; heaven forbid – the car was king and we were its servants.

Today, they call the concept of placing almost everything you could want within walking distance New Urbanism. But it's not a new idea.

Back in the '60s, I flew over the nearly 28,000 acres that Walt Disney Productions had just acquired. I looked out the window of the company's Gulfstream as Walt described to me what would be built there.

He was most excited about the Experimental Prototype City of Tomorrow (EPCOT): a living community, with lots of pedestrian paths and greenery, jobs within walking distance of homes, a place where corporate America could test its latest inventions, and buildings designed to support the human spirit, not overwhelm it.

Walt died in December 1966, before his vision could be realized; sadly, EPCOT was turned into a sort of permanent World's Fair.

A February 2, 1967, news release from Disney announced what EPCOT was to be. It quoted Walt from his last film, a 25-minute introduction to his concept: "I don't believe there's a challenge anywhere in the world that's more important to people everywhere than finding solutions to the problems of our cities. But where do we begin? Well, we're convinced that we must start with the public need. And the need is not just for curing the old ills of old cities. We think the need is for starting from scratch on virgin land like this, and building a community that will be a prototype of the future."

Walt would have loved Larchmont Village or Old Pasadena (just look at Disneyland's Main Street USA). Instead, we've got the terminal kitsch of the Seven Dwarfs serving as pillars on his Burbank lot and very little that is people-scale or people-friendly across the Valley he called home.

So our suburbs keep sprawling and nothing matters but low-density housing that drives people from their homes onto the freeway to distant jobs in ugly buildings.

And then we have our office buildings.

All across the Valley we work in rectangular blocks of concrete and rebar with skins of reflective black glass or some other cold materials, with but one imperative: get as many rentable square feet on the land as possible. And of course, build them as tall as the zoning will allow.

Cole Porter wrote "Don't Fence Me In" in 1942. Well, we've gone and fenced ourselves in with miles of concrete freeways and roadways, undistinguished office buildings and shopping malls, and a near-total disregard for the beauty that comes from preserving and restoring old buildings.

In England, instead of demolishing old buildings, they support the brick façade while they create a totally new building behind it. Our approach is to take the lovely La Reina Theater in Sherman Oaks and turn it into another glorified strip mall or to replace the historic Ambassador Hotel with a school.

Is it too late to do anything about the mess we've made of things when it comes to urban design, planning, and architecture in the Valley?

Mayor Villaraigosa will soon be naming a new planning director for Los Angeles.

We need a planning director who can do two things:

- Create a vision for our city and generate support from all constituencies.

- Direct the Planning Department to a new way of thinking. As one of our City Councilmen whispered to me at a recent meeting of elected officials, "We need a Planning Director who will kick butt!"

I wish I lived in that Valley Councilman's district so I could vote for him. We need to get tough on out-of-compliance signs and signs that remain after a tenant vacates a commercial building.

We need to make it worthwhile and laudable to turn an ugly building into one that is pleasing to the eye and beckoning to the shopper.

We need our chambers of commerce, neighborhood councils, and homeowners' associations to take a leading role in assuring that what we create enhances our communities. I'm not advocating that they have the right to play Roman emperor and go thumbs up or thumbs down on projects, but why don't those organizations and the Economic Alliance recognize and honor those who renovate, repair, and rebuild their properties and those who create visually interesting new ones?

The Encino Chamber of Commerce, like other organizations, once gave an award for the most distinguished buildings and developments; they don't anymore.

No surprise. There is not much worthy of it. We can change that.

***

> We shape our buildings; thereafter they shape us.
> —Sir Winston Churchill

Valley Residents, Firms Returning Favor

I was wrong.

Last month I wrote that the San Fernando Valley was ugly. I take it all back.

Yes, the buildings may be uninspiring and lacking in architectural interest, but what really counts are the people...and they are beautiful.

That was never made more obvious than our Valley business community's response to the devastation wrought by Hurricane Katrina.

Dozens of Valley companies are creating matching gifts programs, making in-kind donations, providing collection points for funds, and writing company checks. The outpouring has been so spontaneous and generous that it would take pages to acknowledge every significant donation. Just a few worth noting:

- California State University Northridge (CSUN), one of the Valley's five largest employers, raised in excess of $85,000 from its students, faculty, and staff.

- Most of our large shopping malls and supermarkets provided facilities for their customers to make hurricane relief donations.

- Clay Lacy Aviation had several of their planes delivering relief supplies, and several of the aviation firms at the Van Nuys Airport raised funds for Katrina survivors.

- Galpin Motors donated $10,000 and has arranged for employee contributions. A van with half a dozen volunteers has arrived in the Gulf and will stay there indefinitely.

- Local employees at Time Warner are adopting affected families of fellow employees in the devastated area and are sending them purchase cards so that those in need can buy whatever they personally need.

- Local restaurants, such as Vitello's and Santoro's, are donating all or portions of dinner checks to relief efforts.

- Westmed Ambulance Service has five ambulances, a support unit, and a supervisory unit participating in the New Orleans rescue operations for victims of Hurricane Katrina.

- Keyes Automotive donated $100,000 itself, and is leading a campaign to raise additional funds from neighboring businesses.

- Amgen contributed $2.5 million to the Red Cross, and is working on providing additional assistance with medications for those in need.

- Kaiser Permanente, Northrop Grumman, HealthNet, and many other firms headquartered or with major facilities here have made significant contributions.

But our friends at the Mouse House may be responsible for raising more money for Katrina's survivors than any other Valley-based firm, partially because of their ability to reach the public through their media holdings. Disney immediately contributed $2.5 million toward relief: $1 million to the Red Cross' efforts, $1 million to rebuilding programs, and $500,000 to the Points of Light Foundation's Volunteer Center National Network.

In addition, Disney sent televisions, DVD players, videos, books, and games to shelters in six states, and raised millions through on-air telethons and fund-raising activities of its radio and television stations. Los Angeles-based ABC television and radio stations alone have raised more than $2 million through telethons and other activities.

And, of course, Mickey Mouse and other Disney characters began visiting shelters in the affected areas.

(Editorial disclaimer: Many moons ago I was the advertising and promotion manager at Disneyland; in fact, I sometimes traveled with Walt Disney. Tipping my tattered mouse ears to his company will – no doubt – raise its stock significantly, allowing me to retire early, based on my holding of 147 shares.)

A bit over a decade ago, we suffered what was – up until this disaster – the most costly catastrophe in our nation's history, the Northridge Earthquake.

Like many of you, I was involved in helping deal with the results of the temblor.

But what we had to deal with was nothing compared with what the residents of the Gulf States have had to contend with and will deal with for years to come.

Somehow, there's a certain symmetry to the aid the Valley is sending to those stricken by Katrina, because only eleven years ago, we were the recipients of a similar outpouring from the rest of the nation.

The story of Hurricane Katrina is not just about a few hundred looters, poor coordination among government agencies, and flattened buildings. It is also the story of how Americans – once again – have proven themselves to be the most generous people on earth ... and we in the Valley can take pride in doing our share.

Few of us in our business community will ever meet any of those people who are totally bereft of material possessions in the stricken states, but be assured that your generosity is doing wonderful things for fellow Americans in need – and for us.

***

Think of giving not as a duty but as a privilege.
—John D. Rockefeller, Jr.

City Council Needs to Rethink Its Priorities

Probably my favorite thing about the *Los Angeles Times* is its headlines, often pithy, excruciatingly punderful, and sometimes gutsy.

Take these headlines that appeared two weeks ago over an article about some of our City Council goings on: *"Resolved: Reduce Council Puffery"* and *"Curbing Nonessential Blather at City Council."*

Puffery? – Blather? Is that *our* City Council the *Times* is writing about? It certainly is.

Seems two of our Valley City Council members, Greig Smith and Jack Weiss, have had enough of the Council's time being taken up by such essential business as honoring young actors whose credits start and end with one sitcom, television personalities whose particular skill is sharing today's weather with us, and two firefighters who don't pursue just treed cats, but wandering alligators. A tip of the (rarely doffed) hat to both of them.

There is no doubt that spending a morning in the Council's chambers is not likely to fill one with a rush of pride watching democracy in action.

Council members and their staffs chat while citizens are at the microphone addressing issues. Sometimes those comments are worth hearing, sometimes not. But in all cases, those speaking have taken the time and made the effort to participate in our system.

What with the sometimes-fruitless search for a missing Council member needed for a quorum, the incessant cell phone use by members' staffs, or a Council member's imperative to instant-message someone somewhere, our fifteen Council representatives often do the right thing...but just take too long doing it.

Along with several other Valley businesspeople, I recently trekked down to City Hall to testify against the proposed half-cent sales tax increase to fund more police.

For more than two hours, we waited and watched while Los Angeles' fifteen finest commemorated our City's establishment of sisterhood with a certain Central American capital. We heard speeches from that small nation's economic and trade officials, consul, and others. We stood while that country's national anthem was played, and applauded after being treated to a performance by native dancers.

And of course, nearly every Council member had to comment on the earth-shattering benefits of this new international alliance. And then we had to hear the whole thing again from those Council members who could demonstrate their linguistic facility with Spanish!

After two hours of international goodwill, the Council took up the issue of a sales tax increase.

The debate was heated, with Council member Perry pointing out how minimally the sales tax increase would hurt, whereas her Valley counterpart, Council member Zine (who was later proven to be accurate) expressed confidence that money for police officers could be found within the existing budget.

When it was time for public comment, Council member LaBonge remarked how he really wanted to hear what those who had signed speaker cards had to say. So he walked to the public microphone and placed his hand on the back of one speaker after another, and gave each one thirty seconds to address the issue.

So, speaking on behalf of one of the Valley's leading business organizations, I had thirty seconds to explain why we opposed the proposed sales tax increase. I would have been given more time had I sung a Salvadorian folk song celebrating city-sisterhood.

Don't get me wrong: I'm happy our City Council retains its human touch, honoring many events, people, and organizations. We applaud Council member Smith's plan to allow Valley people to engage in two-way televised conversation with the Council on matters of interest from Van Nuys City Hall...That's the type of convenience and involvement that will help diminish the alienation between the Solons of Spring Street and the populace they represent.

I don't agree with the Consummate Curmudgeon Calvin Coolidge that "After all, the chief business of the American people is business."

There's no intimation from this corner that our City Council members don't work hard, what with committee meetings, constituent issues, studying reports, and the like. In fact, most of them are among the hardest-working people I know, and there are several of them whom I have gotten to know, like, and respect very much.

But Greig Smith and Jack Weiss have got it right. City Council meetings are that body's face to the world. There's no call here for doing away with recognizing that which merits it. But perhaps we could see a little less time spent on the near-trivial and more on dealing with our community's very substantial problems, from trash to taxation to traffic.

I'm glad we have a new Central American sister city... but I'd like back the two hours I spent memorializing it.

***

> *It has been said that democracy is the worst form of government except all the others that have been tried.*
> *—Sir Winston Churchill*

Bullish on the Valley, but Russia Is a Bear

There's not much comparison between the San Fernando Valley and Russia.

Having just returned from ten days in Saint Petersburg and Moscow, I don't presume to be an expert on the politics, system of government, societal nuances, or much else about Europe's largest country, but, to quote Dorothy in *The Wizard of Oz,* "There's no place like home."

A smile is a very precious commodity in Russia. It must be so, because there are so few of them. In the Valley, even the people who dislike you occasionally smile at you...and those who like you do so even more frequently.

And then there's the political system. Don't believe for a minute that the Russian definition of democracy is the same as ours. Although *Business Journal* alternate-issue columnist Greg Lippe and I often rail at the ineffectiveness, inaction, and inattention of elected officials and bureaucrats when it comes to our business community, it's nothing compared with doing business in what is often called The-Former-Soviet-Union.

Bribery of public officials in Russia is so rampant it's an accepted practice and even a prerequisite to doing business. Here, I've been unsuccessful in just bribing myself into a guest parking space in City Hall parking when visiting one of our Valley City Council members. Admittedly, a $5 Baskin-Robbins gift certificate may have been insufficient to tempt the City Hall parking attendant.

And then there are the police...In Moscow, on at least twenty occasions I saw police motion drivers over to the side of the road, not for any infraction, but simply to "check their identity papers." I asked several people if that was accepted practice, and was informed that random police checks of the populace was standard procedure.

I was looked at in near-disbelief when I said that such action, without probable cause, was illegal in our country. Whoever heard of carrying "identity papers" – other than a driver's license – with you at all times? In Russia no one leaves home without them.

Coming out of a Russian Metro station one morning, I saw a beefy policeman roughing up a slight teenage boy. I don't know his infraction, but he wasn't resisting or fighting back as the much larger officer of the law was punching and kicking him. Passersby just looked away. Somehow, I don't think anyone will be filing police brutality charges.

Here in the Valley, other than my occasional brush with the law for exceeding the speed limit by a bit (I'm sure it's because I drive a burgundy Jaguar), I've never been stopped by the police...with the exception of the time that then-Deputy Chief Mark Kroeker put his red lights on and pulled me over to set a lunch date.

And Valley real estate developers, architects, contractors, and designers: I take it (almost) all back. I've maligned our Valley hardscape, but the Valley's buildings are beautiful compared to the Soviet-era construction in Moscow. Describing them as featureless blocks of rectangular granite and cement makes them sound more interesting than they are.

Don't get me wrong.

I'm not the kind of traveler who compares where I'm visiting to what's back home. I enjoy the local cuisine, revel in the history and culture of whatever country I'm in, try (usually unsuccessfully) to speak a few words in the local language, and generally work my tail off not to be the Ugly American from the book of the same name that William Lederer and Eugene Burdick wrote in 1958.

Yes, the Czarist palaces are palatial, the Russian Orthodox churches are beautiful, the history is fascinating, and there are many other reasons to visit Russia. But I didn't find an equivalent to Brent's Deli, Barnes & Noble, or Griffith Park. There *was* a Starbucks knock-off chain (green circle logo and all), but that didn't earn any points with me.

I guess I have to admit it; I'm just a Valley boy.

Winston Churchill's Cold War comment that "Russia is a riddle wrapped in a mystery inside an enigma," may have been true back then, but of more importance today is that doing business and living in Russia is nothing for which I'd trade our lifestyles.

And the next time I complain too stridently about life in our little north-of-Mulholland part of the world, I invite readers to mail me a copy of this column and to remind me that, however bad it may be here, it's better than almost anyplace else.

∗∗∗

> *Russia will not soon become, if it ever becomes, a second copy of the United States or England - where liberal values have deep historic roots.*
> —Vladimir Putin
> President of Russia

Trying to Get a Read on News Rack Mess

Last week, as I was driving down Ventura Boulevard in Encino, I noticed an elderly man sweeping the street in front of his retail store.

I'm not sure why, but I automatically flashed on a simpler time, when shopkeepers took pride not only in their stores, but the sidewalks in front, knowing instinctively that the pedestrian walkway was sort of their welcome mat.

I also thought of a wonderful photograph I've seen of a young Harry Truman sweeping the sidewalk in front of his soon-to-be-bankrupt haberdashery in Independence, Missouri.

Today, of course, our shopping malls have tractor-like machines with bristles resembling giant electric toothbrushes swirling the dirt around and, we presume, into some hidden receptacle. Smaller retailers have the handyman use one of those infernal blowers... doesn't clean up any dirt, but blows it into the street.

And, worst of all, there are those who don't really believe we live in a desert and think that water has no better use than to wash down the sidewalks in front of their stores (my holiday wish for them is outrageous DWP water bills throughout 2006).

Marvin Braude, who served on our City Council for more than three decades, would have been the first to decry – and try to outlaw – noisy blowers and water-wasting shopkeepers. He died earlier this month, and not enough of us pay him the homage he earned. He recognized the dangers of smoking, the value of bike paths and exercise, and the need for green spaces. He tried to do something about all of these issues.

Then I began to wonder what Marvin would have thought of the army of news racks that clutter those same sidewalks.

You know, those racks that offer periodicals ranging from the respectable general-circulation newspapers to those crammed with careers, cars, and classifieds.

These are the same racks that make it difficult for people to emerge from cars; that take up our tax-dollar-created sidewalks for their commercial benefit; that make it difficult to get to parking meters; and that are strategically placed at bus stops, impeding boarding or exiting. I pray the city doesn't allow news racks at Orange Line stops!

When our City Council first began looking at regulating these racks that seem to propagate overnight, those who owned them wrapped themselves, not unexpectedly, in freedom of speech and freedom of expression. It was as if the very foundations of democracy would crumble if we could no longer obtain *Apartment Magazine, Cars Weekly, LA X-Press, Single,* or *Trade Express*, from these racks of many colors.

Don't get me wrong, as a former journalist and editor, I firmly believe that a free press is one of the pillars of our democracy. But because a commercial venture produces a product that is ink on paper doesn't automatically qualify it as part of our news media. These are advertising circulars designed to make a profit (not that there's anything wrong with that, as Jerry Seinfeld would have quipped), with no pretension of providing news, commentary, analysis, or the other elements of what we consider a newspaper.

An ordinance to regulate these news (and in most cases, the word "news" is used lightly) racks was passed in mid-2004. It required publishers with racks to obtain a city permit. The regulation went into effect January 19, 2005.

In March, the Bureau of Street Services, Investigation and Enforcement Unit of the Public Works Department, was still working on the process for publishers to apply for a permit that would allow up to four racks every 100 feet.

But just try, as I have, to find out exactly how many racks have been removed, how many permits have been issued, and when out-of-compliance racks will be cited and/or forced to be dismantled. No luck.

One explanation was truly fascinating: the Street Use Department is waiting for the City's Information Technology Department, which can't seem to get the program for the GPS system to work. Why do we need a Global Positioning System to get rid of news racks, you may ask? Simple, we need to use satellite systems to track where each rack is!

Let me help. Here's a brief catalog of just a few locations in the Valley. There are:

- 26 news racks on Petit Street just south of Ventura Boulevard, in Encino;

- 19 in front of the Post Office at Van Nuys City Hall on Van Nuys Boulevard and Delano Street;

- 10 at Vanowen Street and Reseda Boulevard, in Tarzana, several of them blocking access to parking meters;

- 18 on Reseda Boulevard just south of Ventura Boulevard, in Reseda, eight of them abandoned; and

- A disgusting, and perhaps record-breaking, 57 racks on the north side of Ventura Boulevard between Canoga Avenue and Topanga Canyon Boulevard in Woodland Hills!

There you are guys; go get rid of them...No need to wait for technology to proceed. Why not start with those that are empty and abandoned?

I really like the elderly man who was sweeping his sidewalk; I don't like those who clutter our sidewalks with news racks very much at all.

***

Don't foul the footpath.
—Sign posted on many London streets

Be Resolute in Helping Valley Business

January is the month to take stock of how we fared in 2005 (pretty darn good in our Valley, according to the San Fernando Valley Research Center at CSUN and others), and to delude ourselves about how well our businesses will do in 2006.

It's also the month of New Year's resolutions. And so, here are our five resolutions for Valley business for this year:

Business Can Be Better. A lot of business leaders and writers bemoan the fact that government overregulates us, the media demonizes us, unions bully us, etc. Perhaps we should acknowledge that we have our own imperfections: Enron, Bernie Ebbers, excessive perks and bonuses hidden from shareholders, denied product defects. Let's admit our own failings...and our criticisms of others will have more credence.

Let's work harder to provide exemplary customer service, to offer the best possible value for money, and to hold ourselves to a higher standard of business ethics...that's not only good for Valley consumers, it's good for Valley business.

Give, Without Expecting To Get. Winston Churchill said it best (of course, I'm prejudiced): "You make a living by what you get; you make a life by what you give." Too many of us salve our consciences and feel we meet our commitment to our society by simply writing a check.

There are so many organizations in the Valley that work to meet so many needs that it is impossible to ignore them...so don't. Read to the visually impaired; provide your organizations' products or services at a reduced cost or fee to not-for-profits (as our firm does); give your time to a youth organization; adopt a school; or, even better, come up with your own idea. Many businesses have a single corporate philanthropy; should you?

Pride Isn't Just For Lions. Many years ago, Chicano pride became the byword of Latinos just beginning to emerge from a cloud of official and unofficial discrimination. Then came Black pride and Gay pride; now it's time for Valley business pride. We need to demonstrate our pride in what Valley business contributes to society. We have allowed Westsiders and Downtowners to relegate the Valley to second-class citizenship. Only we can change that.

Let's make 2006 the year in which we express pride in the Valley, including our own businesses, organizations, opportunities, educational institutions, and everything else that makes up our quality of life. It's time to knock the chips from our own shoulders.

We Must Show Elected Officials We're Not "Fowl" Balls. The business community has to do a better job this year of convincing elected officials and their staffs that business is not a sitting duck but the goose that lays the golden eggs of our economy. Everyone in City Hall mouths the words "business friendly," but with labor union supporters predominating in City

Council, and a mayor whose background is in union organizing, business has to be even more vigilant in identifying and advocating on behalf of its interests – which are the interests of the community.

We're the first to congratulate the Council for its initial steps in business tax reform...but there's a lot more to do. Calvin Coolidge was on the mark when he said that, "The chief business of the American people is business." We should expect government to support it.

We Can't Win If We Don't Play. Business leaders must run for positions on neighborhood councils; serve on city commissions; and work harder to become a political force. We can't win the game if we sit on the sidelines. The successes of the labor movement in Los Angeles have proven that point in the last decade.

Business has to use the ballot box to its advantage. Support candidates and issues...with time, money, and enthusiasm. The recent failure of the Governor's business-friendly legislation shows what happens when we sit on the sidelines, or when we fail to use the same tools of communication and persuasion on the electorate that we do on our customer base.

And we need to energize and galvanize our employees, as well. When businesses lose money, the workforce is reduced, and jobs are lost. Business owners and decision makers have to do a better job demonstrating to employees that supporting business issues is good for them.

* * *

An editorial update: Our last column reported on the proliferation of (often not) news racks along many of the Valley's boulevards. Our personal tally showed 26 racks at the corner of Petit Street and Ventura Boulevard in Encino. We don't know if the bureaucracy mavens read the *SFVBJ*, but we're pleased to report that 25 of the 26 racks on that corner have been removed; only *USA Today* has refused to take theirs down. Oh, the power of the press!

***

It's easy to make a buck. It's a lot tougher to make a difference.
—Tom Brokaw

Lonely at the Top
But Often Lucrative

No one ever admits they're wrong anymore.

Have you ever noticed how rare it is for labor unions to admit when their own tactics are over the top? Or for media pundits to discuss publicly (other than in their own trade journals) the reasons for their diminished reputation for objective reporting? Or for elected officials to regulate lobbyists' influence over legislation and government largesse?

Not that there's anything wrong with that.

So, not fearing to go where fools rush in, I dare to use this space in a business publication to write about executive compensation. Oh, I'm not talking about those members of management teams who make $100,000, $250,000 or $400,000 a year – I'm talking about the *really* big bucks.

The SEC has just proposed a series of restrictions and mandated disclosures of executive compensation and pension plan grants. Seems like the federal government might actually mandate what boards of directors should have been enforcing all along.

One of the biggest knocks on business generally is the outsized compensation packages bestowed upon corporate leaders. Government officials and the media love trumpeting the outlandish packages some executives take home. They forget the long hours, including weekends; the fact that businesses rise and fall based on those executives' decisions; the burden of dealing with numerous constituencies; and the many other challenges.

But let's face it, some corporate leaders are getting fat (monetarily, and perhaps even physically) when their companies are struggling and layoffs of good people are implemented.

Here are the top five Valley-based public companies' CEO compensation packages for 2004, according to the *SFVBJ*'s most recent Book of Lists. Any of these seem excessive to you?

- Angelo R. Mozilo (Countrywide Financial Corp.): $23,187,000

- R. Chad Dreier (Ryland Group, Inc.): $19,858,000

- Michael D. Eisner (Walt Disney Co.): $8,312,000

- Mark R. Goldston (United Online): $6,518,000

- Larry C. Glasscock (Wellpoint Health Networks): $5,599,000

Mr. Mozilo, reported the *Los Angeles Times*, is also eligible for an executive pension that will be worth up to $3 million a year for life.

In just the past few weeks, the *Los Angeles Times*, the *Wall Street Journal*, *Fortune* magazine, and many more, have published lengthy articles on how out of whack the compensation of senior American executives is, compared both to those of other nations and of our own workforce.

Options, pensions, a broad array of perks...these all add up to packages that shareholders know about... and almost never have an opportunity to approve.

Last month, the *Wall Street Journal* reported that the ratio of the average Fortune 500 chief executive to that of the U.S. President's salary in 1960 was two-to-one. Today, it is thirty-to-one. I don't think our Presidents have gotten any worse, but I also don't think our corporate leaders have gotten any better.

The average American CEO's salary is 475 times greater than the average worker's. "In Japan," the *Journal* reports, "it is 11 times greater; in France, 15 times; in Canada, 20; in South Africa, 21; in Britain, 22."

Are our CEOs really more than 20 times more effective than those of Great Britain?

Of course, there are many executives who have their compensation tied to the success of the company.

General Motors' CEO just announced that he is cutting his salary by 50 percent (but don't worry, he's not living in a Detroit homeless shelter yet). Another approach is that of John Mackey's, CEO of Whole Foods Markets, who limits his pay to no more than 14 times that of his average employee.

So, what's the point of it all? Well, as long as boards of directors are willing to pay outrageous salaries to their senior executives; as long as CEOs can avoid having shareholders know how much they're taking home (or should it be "mansion"?); and as long as the SEC lets those executives hide pensions, perks, and Porsches, the situation won't improve.

There's another problem with off-the-charts compensation packages: they have become the most visible and obvious example of executive greed. And no one enjoys positioning outsized executive salaries as the jutting tip of an iceberg of corporate excess more than media columnists, anti-business bloggers, elected officials, and others who need a convenient scapegoat for business generally.

I'm not against big salaries for those who earn them and deserve them. I'm against the rewarding of mediocrity at the top, the opportunity these excessive salaries provide to those who criticize all business, and I'm against leaders of public companies who don't remember that we – the ones who buy the stock – are the *real* owners of the businesses.

There is hope, however. Just last week the *Wall Street Journal* reported that boards of directors may be paying attention to the outcry over inflated – and often inappropriate – compensation. According to the *Journal's* research, last year 30 of 100 major U.S. corporations based a portion of their CEO's compensation on meeting performance targets, up from 23 in 2004 and 17 in 2003.

Maybe we should all work toward relating senior executives' compensation – here in the Valley and across the nation – to the success of their enterprises.

By the way, Angelo, my grande nonfat latte at my Encino Starbucks has gone up from $3.05 to $3.15 – brother, can you spare a dime?

**

Executive compensation is the acid test of corporate governance.
—Warren Buffett
Investor

Bookworm's Homage to the Printed Word

The Knight Ridder newspaper chain sells out; staff reductions continue to decimate the *Los Angeles Times*; while newspapers everywhere are pitied as dinosaurs on the edge of an economic extinction wrought by television, the internet, and computer games.

...And yet, my passion for print endures.

It probably started when I was editor of the Mark Twain Junior High School *Riverboat*. Although my student journalistic career blossomed with editorships of the Venice High School *Oarsman* and the UCLA *Daily Bruin*, it was really my high school print shop that injected copious amount of printers' ink into my veins. More than once, my digits came perilously close to being separated from the rest of my hand by the incessant movement of a now-antiquated platen press.

In a UCLA journalism class, Professor Robert Rutland disputed my assertion in my first essay that the still-published *Connecticut Courant* had a circulation of 8,000 in the Revolutionary War era. "Couldn't be," he chastised me, "there wasn't enough newsprint to produce that many copies of any newspaper in the mid-eighteenth century; where did you get that mistaken idea?"

I told him I couldn't remember where I read it, but I was confident that I was right. He threw down a pedagogic challenge: "You don't have to take any more tests for the rest of the year; just turn in one paper at year end defending your 8,000 circulation figure. If you convince me, you'll get an A for the course; if not you'll get a D."

My semester-long quest for the truth resulted in the discovery that the newspaper publishers' wife was the daughter of a wealthy Canadian who owned huge tracts of timber...source of more than enough paper for a circulation of 8,000 – and an A for me!

Until recently, books and newspapers had always been more important to me than magazines. That is, until late last year, when United Air Lines informed me that I had amassed sufficient frequent-flyer miles for a round trip to Indio, and wouldn't I like to receive some terrific magazines to use up those miles?

Sounded like a good deal to me (I was never a big fan of Indio, except for the date milkshakes), so I signed up...and now I'm inundated: the *Wall Street Journal, Daily Variety, Fortune, Forbes, Fast Company, Time, The Economist*, and several more. I sometimes feel I get more magazines than the owner of the newsstand just off Ventura and Topanga Canyon Boulevards in Woodland Hills.

As a result, my professional productivity has dwindled to a fraction of its pre-magazine-subscription level, but boy, am I ever smarter!

I'll probably let them all run out, except for *The Economist*. How can you not love a periodical whose inside masthead proclaims: "First published in September 1843 to take part in a severe contest between intelligence, which presses forward, and an unworthy, timid ignorance obstructing our progress"?

A 163-year-old magazine, and I know of no better coverage of what's going on in the world today. Here's your tip of the week from the *SFVBJ*: buy a copy and see if you love this periodical as much as I do.

...And then there are the books.

I still have my Illustrated Junior Library volumes, one of them inscribed by my mother: "For Marty's sixth birthday." And the collection keeps growing. I'm up to something over 2,000 books, with no end in sight.

Ray Bradbury, David McCullough, Charles Kuralt, Israel's Foreign Minister Abba Eban, Studs Terkel, and even O.J. Simpson, who I knew and traveled with, are just a few who have inscribed their books to me. Kitty Kelley signed my copy of her book, *Nancy Reagan: The Unauthorized Biography* and included her home phone number – in case I should ever be in Washington, D.C.!

Except for the smell of the first cup of fresh coffee in the morning or a sip of the finest Napa Cabernet, is there a more satisfying sensory experience than that of opening up a new book for the first time...and the feeling of regret when one turns the last page?

The Barnes & Noble at Hayvenhurst Avenue and Ventura Boulevard and the mail order History Book Club should make me honorary shareholders I've invested so heavily in their products.

But of course, my prized possessions are my rare editions of some of Winston Churchill's works. I love the ever-so-slightly yellowed pages with just a bit of foxing, the leather bindings, the faintly musty odor, the feel of them in my hands…and most of all the words they contain.

So it's no *People*, *Trailer Life*, or *Popular Mechanics* for me. I'm not going to be reading books on my PDA or computer screen. The *New York Times* I read online every morning will never replace the real thing…not even close, particularly on Sundays.

The ancient Pharaohs decreed that they be buried with their greatest possessions, so they could enjoy them in the Afterworld. Makes sense to me.

Bury me with my books…and the current issue of *The Economist*.

***

> *I cannot live without books.*
> —President Thomas Jefferson

School's Out on the Mayor's Plan for LAUSD

Over a pear and walnut salad at Paul's in Tarzana a friend asked me, "Why should the business community care about whether the LAUSD is broken up?"

"We shouldn't," I replied, "except that we're parents as well as businesspeople, children represent the work-force of the future, and we're probably wasting dozens of millions of dollars a year that could be put to better use."

It is a law of nature that the larger the institution, company, or country, the greater the waste. That's why there's greater efficiency in almost any well-run Valley entrepreneurial business than there is in General Motors, and why Switzerland (or fill in the name of any small European nation) is more efficient than the U.S.

If there's anything the Los Angeles Unified School District *isn't*, it's unified…or efficient.

The waste in the District is astronomical – from supplies to manpower. A school bus was dispatched to a North Valley elementary school once with nothing aboard to be delivered but a roll of masking tape that was on back order (that occurrence never made either the media or any LAUSD audit).

Money is allocated to schools in a peculiar fashion. For example, a school may have money for supplies but needs equipment, or the other way around, but funds may not be used for what is needed...only for what is allocated, despite the need.

This year's LAUSD budget is $13,166,864,970...I wonder how much of it is being spent efficiently.

With more than 725,000 students, the LAUSD is the largest in the state and the second-largest in the nation. There are 1,131 schools in the District. As of November 2005, there were 37,026 regular teachers out of a total of 77,754 LAUSD employees. That means that fewer than half of the District's employees actually teach...and how do we all feel about *that*?

And then there are the antagonists, the union in one corner and the District in the other. There is no doubt that the teachers' union, UTLA, is heavy-handed and a bit disingenuous when they say that they only care about the kids. It's equally true that the administration is laden with nonproductive administrators and programming specialists. (The phrase, "A pox on both their houses," springs to mind.)

I have a lot of respect for Superintendent Roy Romer, a hard-working executive who is dealing with a Hydra-headed monster out of control. I'd have a lot *more* respect if he was a little less defensive and a little more willing to admit that he heads a dysfunctional bureaucracy. (Note to self: not that there aren't other dysfunctional bureaucracies in this town.)

Our City Controller, Laura Chick, spoke at VICA's Board of Directors' meeting last week. She reminded those in attendance that she had proposed conducting an independent audit of the District, an offer that was rebuffed out of hand.

She shared the fact that there have been numerous audits of individual programs, but not one of the overall District. She also pointed out that there has been no published follow-up to the audits…an analysis of specific actions taken in response to the audit's recommendations.

Mayor Villaraigosa's clarion call to break up the LAUSD resonates with a lot of people, but it's a bit like Valley secession; we haven't heard all of his details yet.

Laura Chick is like many of us, admitting that she is waiting to "hear the specifics of the Mayor's plan before endorsing it."

On April 18, the Superintendent announced that the District has approved an independent audit conducted by Education Resource Strategies. The LAUSD website reads: "The performance audit will examine the potential for reductions in non-school expenditures, identify other potential savings or efficiencies in the operation of the District and propose long-range strategies for controlling costs so that more resources can be directed to classroom instruction."

This most recent performance review audit will cost the District approximately $324,000.

I have two members of my own family who each spent more than 20 years working for the School District. I stand second to none in my ability to recount horror stories of money wasted; politically correct but educationally disastrous decisions; administrators, teachers, and other staff not even close to qualified to educate our children; and an environment so dangerous it makes the classroom in the film *Blackboard Jungle* seem like an idyllic *Goodbye, Mr. Chips*.

And here's a quote guaranteed to scare the life out of any parent, from the UCLA Health Services Research Center: "The Los Angeles Unified School District (LAUSD) is comprised of 722,000 students, many of whom are at increased risk for exposure to violence and other traumatic events due to increasing community violence and poverty." Great, where can I sign my kids up for an environment like that?

The bottom line is that the LAUSD is much too large to be managed properly, particularly by people who have no business experience. While education must be the District's primary focus, managerial types with business experience should be running the management side of this behemoth.

In reality, the District is a big business as well as an educational institution; people who have been promoted to the top have gotten there through promotions, starting out as teachers and never knowing anything else.

I love the cliché, "If it ain't broke, don't fix it." Well, for those of you who don't realize it, the LAUSD *is* broke, and school's still out whether our peripatetic Mayor can fix it.

But I'm willing to let him give it a try.

***

A mind is a terrible thing to waste.
—United Negro College Fund slogan

Time to Develop a Business Attraction Program

Bruce Ackerman, President and CEO of the Economic Alliance of the San Fernando Valley, is very proud of his organization's Valley of the Stars branding campaign.

He should be.

According to the Alliance's website: "In 1997, the Economic Alliance created the Valley of the Stars name and logo, developing a regional brand campaign for wider exposure for the San Fernando Valley. This has resulted in several major Valley-wide and regional events, co-branded with the Economic Alliance: The Valley of the Stars Fair, Valley of the Stars Heart Run & Walk, and the Valley of the Stars Memorial Day Parade."

Granted, the Valley of the Stars branding campaign has begun to create a sense of one-ness and pride in who we are. It plays a role in diverse activities designed to support business already in the Valley, it provides an umbrella for the Alliance's programs to retain business we have, and it helps bring a sense of connection between our businesses and our communities.

That's the good news.

Here's the bad news: It doesn't – and isn't designed to – bring us new business. And we need to start doing that.

We need to sit up and take notice when the lack of housing gives pause to potential employers researching a location that their employees can afford; when our infrastructure can't accommodate growth, let alone the businesses we have; and when our city and state lawmakers have a reputation (deserved or not) for being business-unfriendly.

The exodus of companies such as the *Los Angeles Times* and Washington Mutual has a significant ripple effect on the area's overall economy. The unheralded relocation of smaller organizations to adjacent municipalities, to other California cities, and even to other states that woo them, such as Nevada, Arizona, and Texas, all negatively impact our economy. (Not that Nevada's nutty 'peanut' economic development campaign would make *me* reach for the phone and call.)

Sadly, we have allowed others to define us: Valley girls, strip malls, post-World War II suburban housing tracts, porn capital of the world, culturally deprived, and much worse. The Valley is also branded with the negatives laid on our entire region: smog, traffic congestion, racial strife, too few police and too many crooks... in short, not a place to move *your* business.

Part of the problem is that the Valley *does* have a good story to tell, we just haven't told it. The weather, availability of an educated workforce, an environment of entrepreneurialism, cultural and ethnic diversity, and other attributes of the area would be attractive to many a company...if only our story were told to them in a compelling fashion.

It's time for us to begin competing in the marketplace of business attraction. We need to create a real strategy and program for business attraction and then implement it. How do we go about it?

- Enlist the involvement of key organizations and individuals in the San Fernando Valley who realize the importance of attracting new business to our Valley and are able to research, plan, and bring a real economic development program to fruition.

- Research why companies that are here chose to establish themselves in the Valley, and determine why they stay here.

- Create the "case," an inventory of reasons to relocate to the Valley, including a determination of which types of industries are most likely to thrive in the area...those are the ones to focus on first.

- Review the "best practices" of other cities and regions in economic development, including an examination of how they have positioned themselves in the marketplace, what materials they create, the activities they implement, and what resources they have committed to such programs.

And it's not inappropriate to ask our Valley City Council members what they have been doing to attract business. After all, more jobs mean more taxes, which allow for more city services, which is what constituents love...and then they vote for those elected officials who provide those services.

We have community service awards, Fernando Awards, Z Awards, chamber of commerce awards...why don't we have awards for achievement in bringing business to the Valley? Maybe we haven't even educated *ourselves* why it's important to do so.

So, why don't all those award-winning Valley leaders and Valley elected officials get together and begin to create a strategy to bring us more business? Leaders of the Economic Alliance clearly recognize the need for a strong business attraction program, and have begun discussing it.

A successful business attraction program will be a great shot in the arm for the Valley's economy and the rest of our business community. Besides, we have the tools to win at that game.

Then we will be able to be proud of a branding campaign in which we can call ourselves: "Valley of the *Business Stars.*"

***

> *The trouble in American life today, in business as well as in sports, is that too many people are afraid of competition.*
> —Knute Rockne
> Notre Dame Football Coach

Time to Develop a Business Attraction Program

(Photo Credit: Los Angeles Valley College Historical Museum)

The *Daily News* has undergone many a name change, but unlike so many other newspapers, it *has* endured. Seemingly alone in a vast tract known as the San Fernando Valley, this is the *Daily News* circa 1912, on Sylvan Street west of Van Nuys Boulevard.

Ten Years – And a Lot Hasn't Changed

I'm not very good at following directions.

Ye Olde Editor of the *Business Journal* asked me to write about how the last ten years in the Valley have changed, as this issue of the *SFVBJ* celebrates its first decade of publication.

The truth is, we've been evolving ever since William Mulholland changed us irrevocably on November 15, 1913.

It was on that day that he stood on a peak at the north end of the Valley and celebrated with the city fathers the completion of the great aqueduct that stretches 233 miles from the Owens River to Los Angeles. Mr. Mulholland (no one ever called him "Bill") looked over the expanse of the Valley, pointed to the water his 5,000 workmen had labored to bring from the north into our region and uttered, "There it is, take it."

And we did.

Of course, I should be following orders and writing about the Valley's demographic changes over the past decade, highlighted by the explosion of the Latino population; the concomitant increase in the number of Latino elected officials; the incessant noise of construction heralding the erection of another office high rise or condo; and the continuing growth of the business community.

And yes, changes have been dramatic. Try to find an orange grove, a full-service gas station, or a shabby motel with paint peeling on its tacky sign flashing in neon green, "Vac ncy."

Ten years ago, David Fleming and Bert Boeckmann were the "Mr. Bigs" of the Valley – they still are (and deserve to be).

A decade ago I was asking for my pastrami very lean at Brent's, confident it had no gastronomic equal among our area's delis. I still ask for my pastrami very lean... and Brent's is still our best deli. And who wouldn't drive the extra mile ten years ago – or today – for breakfast at Millie's?

Lots of other restaurants are here after more than a decade...but we *do* mourn the loss of Diamond Jim's, the steak house at the corner of Sepulveda and Ventura Boulevards; Du-Par's in Encino; and Mary's Lamb in Studio City.

Many of the banks, law firms, and CPA practices we turn to for help in our business lives have been here for more than ten years. Dozens of the social agencies, healthcare facilities, and other not-for-profits that provide assistance to those in need have quietly done their job for years and years.

And how many chambers of commerce have we gained or lost in the last ten years? Not many...if any. In fact, the Woodland Hills Chamber has been around since 1942 and the Encino Chamber since 1936. VICA was founded in 1949, and even that organizational upstart, the Economic Alliance, recently celebrated its tenth anniversary.

Los Angeles Valley College has been graduating young people for our workforce since 1949.

We've been buying our cars from Auto Stiegler since 1951, Galpin Ford since 1946, and Casa de Cadillac since 1948...and been cursing the congested freeways we drive them on for longer than that. And no one would dare say that traffic has been reduced, no matter how many Orange Line buses speed (OK, change that to "proceed cautiously") across the dedicated busway.

Disney's been making movies on the same lot since 1940, while Warner Bros. hasn't moved since 1929, and Uncle Carl Laemmle dedicated Universal City Studios in 1915.

Even smaller companies have called the Valley home for a very long time. Bobrick Washroom Equipment has been cleaning up since coming to the Valley in 1966, while people have been bedding down at Beverly Garland's Holiday Inn since 1973, Clay Lacy Aviation has been flying high since 1968, and Flip's Tire Center has been treading the Valley since 1972.

It's not that the *Journal's* decade in the Valley isn't an accomplishment to be noted. After all, we are certainly underrepresented when it comes to our own media. We've never had our own television station, and except for the late, lamented KGIL, never boasted a major radio station. Even the *Los Angeles Times*, which used to have a significant presence here, clearly places less emphasis on Valley news.

When it comes to media, however, the *Daily News* is the undisputed longevity champion of the Valley. The paper was founded in 1911 as the *Van Nuys Call*, and became, successively, the *Van Nuys News*, the *Van*

Nuys News and Valley Green Sheet, and eventually the *Los Angeles Daily News*.

Communities, like people, tend to change rapidly in their youth, and the rate of change slows with the aging process. Our Valley is changing a little less dramatically now...maybe we're growing up.

The more things change the more they are the same.

***

> *When you're finished changing, you're finished.*
> —Benjamin Franklin

A Very Real Truth – Inconvenient or Not

It's too bad that Al Gore is the focal point of the movie, *An Inconvenient Truth*. He detracts from his own message.

It's not that he does a poor job presenting his new documentary on global warming; in fact, he was less stiff than we've ever seen him. He introduced himself by saying, "I am Al Gore, I used to be the next president of the United States of America," with a wry reference to his own political fortunes.

The problem is, today everything is viewed in light of the excessively partisan political landscape we've drawn. It's not a pretty picture: people are "red" or "blue," "left" or "right," "hawks" or "doves," "pro labor" or "pro business."

And so, unfortunately, as a former vice president and presidential candidate, the film's presenter – and viewers' opinions of him – obscures his own message.

Those who consider themselves environmentalists or conservationists hail *An Inconvenient Truth* as gospel, and a wake-up call to the rest of us. Those who align themselves on the other end of the issue say the movie's scare tactics are based on nothing but unproven scientific bunk.

Al Gore's presence gets in the way of a central fact: This film's topic is not as much a political issue as it is a moral issue.

This is a film that takes on a highly complex issue, and there are rarely simple explanations to complex issues. How do you explain the issue of global warming so that most of us can understand it, and then, if we do, how are we to react to the message?

In some ways, it's pretty simple. You show snow-peaked Mount Kilimanjaro a few years ago, and then its nearly-brown look today; the comparative pictures are striking. You listen to Al Gore intone seriously, "If you look at the 10 hottest years ever measured, they've all occurred in the past 14 years, and the hottest of all was 2005." And that doesn't even count the July heat wave we've all been experiencing here in the Valley.

Business has demonstrated its ability to evolve in light of environmental concerns in the past, and appears ready to do so again.

In 1953, inventor Robert Apblanalp, later one of Richard Nixon's closest friends and financial backers, patented the technology that led to the creation of the spray can. Soon his Precision Valve Corporation was earning more than $100 million annually manufacturing more than one billion aerosol cans each year in the U.S. and a few other nations.

By the mid-1970s, science had demonstrated that the fluorocarbons in those spray cans were adversely affecting the ozone layer, which led to creation of an environmentally friendly aerosol can.

Al Gore should be pleased with the increasing signs that business realizes it has a responsibility for environmental matters, and broad media coverage is pushing that awareness along.

The July 17 issue of *Business Week* features a four-page spread examining how some companies are adapting to the reality of rising temperatures and other climate changes. Recently retired NBC anchor Tom Brokaw is hosting a Discovery Channel program on global warming and says he was impressed by *An Inconvenient Truth*.

In an editorial last week, the *New York Times* referred to a recent National Academy of Sciences report that "the earth is inexorably heating up and that industrial emissions are largely responsible. This is a case of global importance, not least because America's failure to act decisively has discouraged the rest of the world from acting decisively."

It appears that business is getting the message.

The Bob Hope Airport spent $1.3 million installing electric charging stations at all 14 boarding gates to encourage airlines to convert from diesel to electric powered ground service equipment. Southwest Airlines converted over 80 percent of its equipment to electric power after the chargers came on line, and this conversion happened much faster than anyone expected.

Sales of hybrid cars such as the Toyota Prius continue strong, and the new documentary, *Who Killed the Electric Car?* is sure to keep the role of the vehicle in environmental pollution top of mind.

Brian Sobel, Sales Manager of Keyes Woodland Hills Honda, says, "People are willing to spend the $6,000 more for a hybrid than a non-hybrid Civic Honda. If I had 100 on my lot I could sell them all...a good example of the growing awareness of the importance of the environmental issue."

Some Bank of America employees are eligible for a $3,000 cash incentive to buy a hybrid car; they are one of three Fortune 1,000 companies to offer cash incentives to buy a hybrid.

As business people, we have a responsibility to look further than the next quarter's profits. Hackneyed phrases as "giving back to the community" and "corporate responsibility" have to be matched with action. One doesn't have to be an environmental activist to see that our climate is changing at a geometric rate, and that our children and their children will be impacted by decisions we make now.

Go see *An Inconvenient Truth*. You may agree or disagree with Al Gore's politics, but don't let that get in the way of considering his message.

You may – or may not – share his point of view, but you can't walk out of the theater without thinking... and perhaps that is indeed the sign of a good movie, after all.

***

> *Politics aside, I think you owe it to yourself to see this film.*
> —Roger Ebert

Mel and Andy:
Two Birdbrains of a Feather

They couldn't be more different. Yet within the past month, both have run afoul of norms of good behavior.

One is a wealthy and successful producer and director; the other a respected civil rights leader.

One is the star of *Mad Max*, *Gallipoli*, *Lethal Weapon*, and *Braveheart*; the other a former mayor of Atlanta, U.S. Congressman, and U.S. Ambassador to the United Nations. One brought us *The Passion of the Christ*; the other brought the Olympic Games to Atlanta.

And they have both brought us face to face with the sore that has festered and contaminated our country since the framers of the Constitution argued whether women should vote and Black people should be free... and said "no" to both.

Their names are Mel Columcille Gerard Gibson and Andrew Jackson Young, Jr.

On July 28, Gibson was arrested for driving in excess of 85 miles an hour with a blood-alcohol level of 0.12 percent, and proceeded to spew anti-Semitic venom and comments derogatory to women, to put it charitably.

On August 17, Young offered the following diatribe during an interview with the West's largest African American newspaper, the *Los Angeles Sentinel*. When asked if he was concerned that his (now former) employer, Wal-Mart, was forcing mom-and-pop retailers out of business, he said: "...those are the people who have been overcharging us, selling us stale bread and bad meat and wilted vegetables. And they sold out and moved to Florida. I think they've ripped off our communities enough. First it was Jews, then it was Koreans and now it's Arabs."

In the memorable lead-in to an old-time radio program, the announcer asked in a sonorous tone: "Who knows what evil lurks in the hearts of man? The Shadow knows."

We don't know what evil lurks in the hearts of Mel Gibson and Andrew Young, but we do know what came out of their mouths...fear, anger, and hatred of people different than they are. All the carefully-crafted apologies don't erase the words or the revealing thought processes of those who spoke them.

The international furor over their intemperate-at-best remarks forces us to look at our own community.

Let us not forget that the Rodney King tragedy occurred in the San Fernando Valley, that approximately 3,200 Japanese Americans were relocated from the Valley to detention camps during World War II, and that the now-shopworn phrase "white flight" referred to what one blogger on Black N LA referred to as "the lily-white Valley."

But it's a different world now.

It is difficult to write about race relations in our society without being branded either a racist on one hand, or a victim of political correctness on the other. But whether one's politics tilt to the left or the right, there is no denying that the San Fernando Valley has become a truly multicultural, multiethnic, region.

According to the most recent San Fernando Valley Economic Report prepared by CSUN's College of Business and Economics, in 2004 the San Fernando Valley was composed of 62.69 percent Latinos; 22.99 percent non-Latino Whites; 8.85 percent Asian, Pacific Islanders or Filipinos; 4.79 percent African Americans; and a variety of smaller ethnicities.

While the Valley is home to people whose ancestors came not only from Europe, but Asia, Africa, Central and South America, but every other corner of the globe, our business leadership does not reflect that ethnic and cultural diversity.

While organizations such as VICA, the Economic Alliance, several chambers of commerce, and others, have recognized the advantages of more diverse boards, the recognition still far outweighs the achievement.

To the leaders of those organizations: try harder.

To those who would like to be leaders in those organizations: tell them so.

My friend Marc Tapper shared a relevant story: One night an old Cherokee told his grandson about a battle that goes on within us all. He said, "My son, the battle is between two 'wolves' inside each of us. One wolf is Evil. It is anger, envy, jealousy, greed, resentment, inferiority, lies, and superiority. The other wolf is Good. It is peace, hope, love, humility, kindness, benevolence, tolerance, generosity, truth, and compassion."

The young boy thought about it for a minute and then asked his grandfather: "Which wolf wins?"

The elderly Cherokee replied simply: "The one you feed."

Two final thoughts: Loyola University awarded Mel Gibson an honorary Doctor of Humane Letters in 2003. They should ask for it back; he doesn't strike most of us as "humane" at all.

Similarly, President Carter awarded Andrew Young the Presidential Medal of Freedom in 1981. Twenty-five years later he seems to have forgotten that freedom in this country includes Jews, Koreans, and Arabs.

***

By swallowing evil words unsaid, no one has ever harmed his stomach.
—Sir Winston Churchill

A Real Bull Story with a Moral for Business

Does anyone read *Ferdinand the Bull* anymore?

Hitler ordered it burned, while Gandhi called it his favorite book.

For the uninitiated, Ferdinand was the 800-word literary brainchild of Munro Leaf, who wrote the 1935 children's story about a flower-sniffing Spanish bull.

While the other bulls wanted to be selected to fight in the bullring in Madrid, Ferdinand wanted to sit under the cork tree and smell the flowers.

When men came to select the roughest bull to fight in the ring, the other bulls snorted and pawed the earth, so the men would think that they were strong and fierce.

Knowing they wouldn't pick him, Ferdinand went over to his favorite cork tree and sat down, but accidentally sat on a bee and was stung. He jumped up with a bellow and ran around snorting and pawing the ground as if demented. The men shouted with joy, confident they had found the fiercest bull of all. So they took Ferdinand away for the bullfight.

He was promoted as "Ferdinand the Fierce," and when released, he ran into the ring as everyone applauded wildly, because they were sure he would fight fiercely.

But when Ferdinand got to the middle of the ring he saw the flowers in the ladies' hair and he just sat down quietly and smelled.

He wouldn't fight no matter what they did. He just sat and smelled. So they took Ferdinand home, and rumor has it that he is still sitting under his favorite cork tree, very happily smelling the flowers.

Do any of us smell the flowers any more?

We have Blackberrys and Treos and all sorts of technology to keep us in touch with others who want us to work harder and produce more.

How many of us have been offended when we're speaking in a meeting and others are text messaging, rather than listening?

We have cell phones so we're never out of touch. How many of us are stuck behind a laggard on the freeway who is more focused on his or her cell phone conversation than driving appropriately?

Sitting at dinner at Pinot Bistro last week, I saw two nicely dressed couples at the next table. One of the four was carrying on a lengthy business discussion on his cell phone – at past 8 p.m. – while the other three looked around uncomfortably, not saying a word.

How often – on evenings or weekends – do we excuse ourselves with, "I just have to check my email," as if the world would end if we don't read and respond to a message within a few minutes.

We have portable computers so we can refine our charts while flying to business meetings in other cities rather than reading a good book or getting to know a seatmate.

In a VICA meeting last week, one well-respected Valley CEO asked why we couldn't start meetings at 7 a.m., while a second said he'd really like our meetings held at breakfast or lunch (so much for a break from work).

Futurists predicted that we would be working a 20-hour week by the year 2000, with machines doing much of the work for us. The sad truth is that we've turned into the machines, working more hours than ever before.

The cliché that there's no glory in being the richest man in the graveyard is a cliché because it's true.

Business is an important part of all of our lives, but it's not our whole life...and too many of us make it our reason for existence.

We talk, we type, we listen...but how often do we *think*?

How frequently do we look out the windows of our Ventura Boulevard high rises just to look at the mountains? When's the last time you pulled over while zipping along Mulholland at night to look at the Valley's lights? When's the last time you've smelled the flowers...or sent some to someone?

Taking time to smell the flowers is good for you...and that's no bull.

***

Seize the moment. Remember all those women on the Titanic who waved off the dessert cart.
—Erma Bombeck

Marketing Philanthropy: Getting by Giving

So, how generous are we?

Are San Fernando Valley businesses more – or less – philanthropically generous than the rest of the city, the country, and the world?

The concept of charity is somehow inherently contradictory to the precepts of capitalism. People work as hard as they can, often relegating ethics, honesty, and fair play to the back burner, while avarice and a win-at-any-price attitude prevail.

And then – they turn around and donate millions to AIDS relief, the homeless or abused, or to hundreds of other worthwhile causes.

The passage of time has dimmed our collective memory of the excesses of the Robber Barons – Rockefeller, Carnegie, Morgan, and the like. Today we remember their charitable gifts to libraries, universities, and philanthropies. John D. Rockefeller hired one of the founders of the public relations profession, Ivy Lee, who managed Rockefeller's transformation from demon to donor by – among other things – having the tycoon give away dimes to children on the streets of New York.

In our own time, we have gone from excoriating the denizens of Silicon Valley (the first time around) for their lack of charitable giving, to admiring the incomparable giving of Bill Gates and many of his compatriots (this time around).

Not to be outdone, Warren Buffett has pledged to support the charitable giving of the Gates Foundation with his own multi-million-dollar gift. And the mid-September issue of *Fortune* touts the philanthropic success President Clinton has achieved by using his charisma, clout – and (others') cash.

Looking closer to home, I had always thought we Californians were a generous people. But according to several publications, we're not even in the top five among the 50 states in charitable giving.

I was equally sanguine about those of us in the Valley.

After all, we support MEND, Haven Hills, the Child Development Institute, New Horizons, El Proyecto de Barrio, and a host of other local not-for-profits, not to mention the large national organizations.

Most of us could rattle off the names of half a dozen true philanthropists in the Valley's business community – I am privileged to know several of them.

But does it stop there? Some of our larger enterprises – a bank, a healthcare company, a few others – are known for their giving. But can you name many smaller, local firms that have established a reputation for supporting worthwhile causes?

Probably not.

Big companies for years have used the concept of cause-relating marketing to both sell products and polish their image.

"Buy two of our widgets and we'll donate $10 to your favorite charity"; "Open an account and we'll send a donation to the Boys & Girls Club of the West Valley"; or "Shop at our mall stores and we'll support one of these charities..." (followed by a long list).

Well here's (to quote Jonathan Swift) a modest proposal: Why don't all of us who have small and medium-sized businesses take a page from the big guys' books?

In essence, it's just doing well while doing good. Instead of just having a "sale," advertise and promote a donation. Instead of telling us that "it's fun to buy a car" at a certain dealership, give a Valley-based charity $50 for every test drive.

Instead of giving us double airline miles for staying at a certain Valley hotel, donate the second set of miles to a charity's account.

It's easy, it's good for the Valley, and it's good business.

Andy, if you donate a dollar to a Valley charity, I promise to let you keep cutting my hair until I go entirely bald. Bert, if you give $150 to a Valley not-for-profit for every Jaguar you sell, I promise to buy my next one from you (of course I only buy one every decade or so – I still love my XJS). Veronica, if you give $2 for every meal I have at your restaurant, I'll promise to order my Santa Fe salad at least three times a month for the next year.

See, it's good for them, it's good for me...and it's good for the Valley.

After all, as he wrote near the end of his life, Benjamin Franklin believed, "I would rather have it said 'He lived usefully,' than 'He died rich.'"

May that be said of all of us.

✳✳✳

You make a living by what you get,
but you make a life by what you give.
—Sir Winston Churchill

We Get *What* in Return for Four More Years?

So let me get this straight...

We voted to extend the term limits of City Council members because they convinced us that 12 – not merely eight – years in office are necessary to solve the major issues of our region.

Having given them this vote of confidence for their stellar achievements so far, and with the expectation of continued excellence, we can no doubt anticipate significant successes on the part of the Council in reducing traffic congestion, achieving a strategic approach to growth and development, enjoying a streamlining of city services, diminishing the influence of gangs, and eliminating the gross receipts taxes.

In return for these anticipated improvements to our quality of life, effective this coming January, each of these public servants will be compensated with an annual salary of $171,000, a city car, and other perks. And, yes, for those who are wondering, that does make ours the highest-paid City Council members in the nation.

Recently, one of these 15 Council members expressed surprise that Los Angeles continues to be perceived as a city of lawmakers unfriendly to business. Are they clueless?

Late last year, our City Council passed an ordinance targeting large grocery stores. Supermarkets larger than 15,000 square feet were ordered to keep existing employees on the payroll for at least 90 days after an ownership change.

And do they think this will *encourage* large stores to open for business in our Fair City?

No surprise that this ordinance is now tied up in a lawsuit that argues that such a law is discriminatory. And of course, we taxpayers are footing the bill for the defense of this blatantly anti-business ordinance.

And just last week, the Council mandated how much 12 hotels on Century Boulevard near LAX should pay their employees, how to distribute service charges and tips, and when they can replace employees in the event of a sale of the hotel.

Up until now, the city has dictated adherence to its living wage ordinance to companies located on city-owned property or which have a city contract. These hotels fall into neither category: they are located on private property and do not have contracts with the city.

Noted economist Milton Friedman was given the Nobel Prize for economic science and has been a senior research Fellow at the Hoover Institution since 1977. He was awarded the Presidential Medal of Freedom and the National Medal of Science. He summed up the problem as neatly as one could: "The government solution to a problem is usually as bad as the problem."

In an October 30 editorial, our beleaguered *Los Angeles Times* got it right: "That so few members of the Council abide by basic principles of economics is a disturbing indicator of the degree of control that organized labor exerts over city government."

Repeat after us: "Killing jobs does not benefit workers."

Listen up Council: Your union supporters are taking you too far down the road of rules, regulations, and restrictions.

Until now, leaders in the business community have bemoaned the fact that Los Angeles is a union-ruled city…and done little about it. Complaining changes nothing.

So, what's the solution?

I suggest lunch.

A lunch whose attendees will include the presidents or chairs of the Los Angeles Chamber of Commerce, the Central City Association, the Economic Alliance, Latin Business Association, VICA, and perhaps one or two more.

Let the agenda be a simple one: how to create an effective alliance of all of this city's business organizations around the simple concept of supporting business-friendly actions and opposing business-unfriendly actions of our city government.

Yes, that is what many of these groups do now individually, but unilateral action is not getting the job done. On those issues which relate to its viability and growth – and that of our region – business must not only speak as one voice but communicate its benefits to all.

The plan should include means of demonstrating the importance of business to all the citizenry of Los Angeles; educating the employees of every coalition member that their jobs depend on businesses staying here; and showing government and the media that growth depends on businesses locating here.

The only other option is to sit around and watch our local elected officials and their union backers slowly strangle the spirit of entrepreneurialism and business-building that made this region great.

***

That government is best which governs the least.
—Thomas Jefferson

Now We'll be Doing it by the Numbers

I used to think that we were all obsessed with sex, drugs, and rock 'n' roll.

I was wrong; we're obsessed with numbers.

It's official: quantity has won out over quality.

We decide on what films to see based on how they're doing at the box-office – as the media dutifully reports to us each Monday – rather than how good we think they are. We check the weekly TV ratings to see if what *we* watch is "in" or "out." And if I have to hear one more "Top Ten" list of things that happened this year I'll Deep Six the whole list!

When opening for holiday shopping at 9:30 a.m. the other morning, the manager of the Costco at Roscoe Boulevard and Canoga Avenue loudly declaimed to those in line, "I only have 93 Playstation 3s." Pity the 94th mother in line.

And then, of course, there's sports. My New York friend John Goodman lives and dies based on where his beloved Red Sox are in the baseball standings.

I have to admit it was nice to see that it was their index fingers UCLA basketball fans were displaying last week, not another digit, to designate their number one standing.

But some numbers really are important (OK, being the number-one basketball team in America *is* important).

December 7 is a date that, as President Roosevelt told us, "will live in infamy." When it comes to World War II, that is certainly true, but when it comes to the Valley's progress, it was a very good day indeed. It was the day that the U.S. Census Bureau, for the very first time, revealed statistics related to – us.

That's right, we're now a separate statistical district. Roughly, the nation's newest statistical district is that portion of Los Angeles north of Mulholland Boulevard, plus the cities of San Fernando, Burbank, Glendale, Calabasas, and even a bit of county land. And those of us who have used the line, "If the Valley was a separate city, we'd be the sixth-largest in the nation," now have to change it to "the fifth-largest in the nation." Because with a population of 1.74 million, the San Fernando Valley is behind only New York, Los Angeles, Chicago, and Houston.

Based on the Census Bureau's first look at the Valley, it is clear that this region has morphed dramatically from being a white, middle-class suburb of Los Angeles to a particularly diverse area. More than 40 percent of us are foreign-born.

According to the statistics released this month, 61.4 percent of the Valley is made up of white residents, 41.6 are Latino, 10.9 percent are Asian, and 4.3 percent are African-American. While that adds up to 118.2 percent, the Census Bureau explains that individuals could register under more than one category...meaning that a whole lot of us identify ourselves as a member of more than one of the four groupings.

How much more diverse could a community be?

No longer merely a bedroom community for commuters who live here but work (that dreaded phrase) "over the hill," the Valley is a job generator, and a potent – and important – one at that.

Perhaps most surprising is how similar we are to the rest of the city. Yes, our median household income is higher than the rest of the city's ($51,717 vs. $42,667); 52 percent of our residents are homeowners compared to the city's 40 percent; and only(!) 12.9 percent of us are below the poverty level, compared to a shocking 20.1 percent in the city. But in most categories, there is great similarity.

The push for a separate census designation is a direct outgrowth of the secession movement. It's sort of a sop: "You can't be a separate city, but we'll give you separate numbers."

But why should we care?

The real answer is, it doesn't matter at all – unless we use these numbers to benefit ourselves.

Now our elected officials can fight for funding for Valley transportation, social services, affordable housing, tax-incentive empowerment zones, and other government monies, based on the Valley being a distinct entity.

Now we can provide businesses considering relocating to the Valley with real numbers regarding our well-educated and experienced workforce. We can prove that we have more than 107,000 residents with graduate or professional degrees and an additional 227,000 with bachelor's degrees. "Businesses are looking for an educated workforce," Congressman Brad Sherman correctly points out.

Beyond that, according to Professor of Economics Dan Blake, Director of the San Fernando Valley Economic Research Center at CSUN, businesses can look at the characteristics of the area and see that this is a market that has a large middle-class, lots of homeowners, and a fluid population – 13 percent of us move each year. Marketers, he says, can tailor their goods and services to who is actually here.

Now we can prove that the San Fernando Valley is a diverse, vibrant, economically viable, and demonstrably important region...with or without the rest of Los Angeles.

Hooray for...us!

***

We're not in Kansas anymore, Toto.
—Dorothy, in *The Wizard of Oz*

It's What's Next That Counts in the Valley

"Whither" is one of my favorite words.

It has that slightly snooty air that accompanies an upper class British accent. It bespeaks to the excitement of not knowing what is yet to be discovered in an unknowable tomorrow. It asks the question: "What's next?"

When it comes to the future of our San Fernando Valley, it's what's next that counts.

What's next for a transportation system that frustrates, rather than facilitates, our movements without and within our region?

Just say the words "101/405 interchange" and a grimace is the universal facial response. Words of an uncomplimentary nature regarding near-gridlock are sure to follow mention of any number of Valley thoroughfares.

We fear to build new homes and communities in outlying areas of Our Valley not only because of the traffic that we generate, but the unmitigated traffic from communities such as Santa Clarita, Lancaster, Palmdale, and other points north and west.

Dealing with our traffic issues is a tall order for the entire city's leadership. The burden falls heavily on the shoulders of Gloria Jeffs, the new General Manager of the city's Department of Transportation.

What's next for the oft-touted but never-delivered regional approach to planning?

In 1853, Napoleon III hired civic planner Baron Georges-Eugene Haussman to transform the ancient French capital of Paris into a modern metropolis. Haussman ruthlessly destroyed blocks of hovels and buildings that stood in the way of creating a wonderful, world-class "City of Light."

Robert Moses was also tasked to nearly rebuild a city. His ambitious public works projects over a 40-year span transformed the urban landscape of New York; he conceived and oversaw the creation of numerous parks, highways, bridges, and buildings. He directed urban renewal projects that resulted in the building of the United Nations' headquarters, Lincoln Center, Shea Stadium, and numerous public-housing complexes. He also created and managed both the 1939 and 1964 World's Fairs.

As Columbia University history Professor Kenneth Jackson wrote, "The achievement of Robert Moses was that he adapted New York City to the twentieth century."

Does our Mayor have the courage to support his new Director of Planning, Gail Goldberg, to do the same, or will we continue to expand in a piecemeal manner?

Will decisions be based on political considerations, or on what is best for our city's future? We need leadership that is creative, visionary, and dynamic. We must replace our patchwork approach to our inevitable growth with a plan that transforms our city into the world's preeminent metropolis. It's too late to give each City Council member near-veto say on projects in his or her area that would impact the entire city.

What's next for Our Valley's ability to really move forward with ethnic and cultural goodwill and harmony?

The southern portion of the Valley is still largely white, while the north is still largely black and brown. As Seinfeld said, "Not that there's anything wrong with that," except that we have to do a better job of communicating with, understanding, and supporting each other. Ignoring the economic disparity that exists between the two sections of Our Valley works to no one's benefit.

We still use divisive words when we should be inclusive. It still rankles when I recall that the head of a well-known social agency in the north end of the Valley called me a racist for deciding to produce a jazz festival in Balboa Park rather than in his preferred location, Hansen Dam.

What's next in Our Valley's relations with the rest of the city?

Yes, we have a mayor who readily acknowledges that there is Life North of Mulholland. And yes, our City Council meets monthly in the Braude Center on Van Nuys Boulevard.

But we continue to receive fewer city services per dollar contributed to taxes than our over-the-hill brethren (that being a geographic, not chronologic, reference to the rest of the city).

And finally...**what's next** when it comes to waking up our business community to the perils it faces?

We have a City Council that has shown they don't shy from mandating what private hotels near the airport should pay their workers; a mayor who is a former union organizer; and a populace that largely thinks business is bad.

Let's hand it to the unions in our city...they've learned that in unity there is strength. That's a lesson business has yet to learn.

What's next for the Valley? It's up to us.

✳✳✳

> *Politics is the art of looking for trouble, finding it, misdiagnosing it and then misapplying the wrong remedies.*
> —Groucho Marx

Dennis P. Zine, who represents the West Valley, is just one of three Councilmembers who voted against another anti-business motion in the City Council.

Labor Wins, Business Loses – Again

Business blinked.

There were more than enough signatures to spare – more than 103,000 – to put the matter to a vote.

But a poll showed that most voters were in support of the "living wage" plan of our union-favoring City Council to force LAX-adjacent hotels to pay about 3,500 workers what the unions thought they should earn. And that led the LA Chamber and other groups to cave.

So, no public vote on the issue.

Instead, last Tuesday the Council voted 9-3 to ever-so-slightly amend the original proposal, and retain the living wage ordinance. The biggest change between the initial and "revised" ordinance is that the city will invest in street and signage improvements, spend $50,000 for a study (ahhh yes, another taxpayer-funded study) to attract new business to the LAX-area "hospitality zone," and a few other goodies, all paid for by us taxpayers, of course.

At least a few key Valley organizations showed up to speak out against the Council's latest anti-business legislation: VICA, UCC, and the Mid Valley and Woodland Hills Chambers.

Hats off to those three Council members (two of them from Our Valley) who voted last Tuesday to oppose this so-called compromise: Bernard Parks, Greig Smith, and Dennis Zine.

Speaking of Councilman Zine, he pointed out to me that even the unions should be against this proposal, since it takes their ability to negotiate out of their hands, and lets the Council decide what workers should earn. Of course, as long as the Council can hand the unions a better deal than they might be able to negotiate on their own, maybe they shouldn't mind.

But the bigger issue is that the Council emerges as giving itself the right to impose its will on private business when it comes to salaries and benefits.

Council member Janice Hahn wins this month's Business Black Hat Award for sponsoring this legislation. She is quoted as saying, in reference to the airport-area hotels, "These workers are not being paid enough currently so the city stepped in." Let's hope Ms. Hahn doesn't decide to tell us that our gardeners, housekeepers, nannies, dental hygienists, and barbers aren't being paid enough either...and that the Council will determine what would be fair compensation for them.

So much for a free market, capitalism, and the law of supply and demand. And, to add irony to insult, the dozen hotels in question are not even in Janice Hahn's district, they're in Bill Rosendahl's.

So, now that the Council has determined that they know better than employers what those employers can afford to pay, here are some potential ordinances we can expect to see floating around City Hall, and wafting out of the offices of certain Council members:

- Since rumor has it that 14.3 percent of the beer brewed at the Valley facility of Budweiser is consumed by city employees, that operation will have to begin paying a living wage immediately.

- Since the productivity of those working near Van Nuys Airport is improved because the sounds of aircraft taking off and landing keeps employees from on-the-job naps, and since the airport is a city facility, those businesses will be subject to a fee commensurate with the improved output of their workforce.

- Since many Los Angeles business owners use city parks, city sanitation services, and city streets, all businesses will be subject to a living wage for their employees.

- Since many Valley workers drive city streets to jobs in the Westside or downtown, any business with Valley residents will be subject to a living wage. Of course, workers who use the 405 or 101 to get Over the Hill will not cause their employers to be subject to this provision, as the freeways are built with state and federal funds.

So what will business do now? Probably spend a few weeks bemoaning how they were had – again – by the unions and City Hall...and wait around for the next blow against the capitalistic system. Or, it can channel its energies into electing better officeholders.

In 1999, when the City Council first passed a living wage ordinance, the business community was promised that the new ordinance would apply only to businesses that chose to do business with the City. To see how well that ordinance has worked, one only has to examine the numbers of competitive bidders on rebuilding Parker Center and the Bradley Terminal – one apiece!

Whoever came up with the slogan "You can't beat City Hall" should amend it to read, "You can't trust City Hall."

***

> *I have come to the conclusion that politics are too serious a matter to be left to the politicians.*
> —Charles De Gaulle

A Modest Proposal to the Successful

As we travel around Our Valley, it's clear that the old saw of "The rich get richer and the poor get poorer" has real meaning.

In the last couple of months, I've visited several of our not-for-profit organizations. I recall:

- Sitting in the reception area of MEND (Meet Each Need with Dignity) in Pacoima, and being struck by the happiness on the faces of the members of a family of five when they were handed a box of food…basic nourishment that they otherwise would not have been able to afford.

- Listening to an eight-year-old tell you that he comes to the Boys & Girls Club of the West Valley because he "feels safe here" reminds us that thousands of Valley children live with fear every day, particularly if their home is in a community terrorized by violent gangs.

- Walking down the aisles of the giant workshop of New Horizons in North Hills and being greeted by big smiles and handshakes from the developmentally disabled who were so pleased to have visitors.

I know that many of our businesses do their fair share – and often more than that – to help individuals and organizations in need.

Being in the public relations profession, I'm eminently familiar with the phrases "cause-related marketing" and "corporate philanthropy." And I'm also familiar with the explanations and excuses: "We've committed our community support budget for the year already"; "we restrict our giving to certain areas, and I'm afraid you don't fit into any of those categories"; and "why don't you apply for a grant from our foundation?"

So, putting on my Robin Hood cap (sans feather), here's my attempt to take just a bit from the (very) rich, and have them give it to the poor:

Not long ago, Pacoima's MEND helped a homeless man who was unemployed and living on the streets. MEND's medical testing showed that, like many poor people, he was diabetic. MEND provided him with insulin and nutritional counseling. Within three months he got a job and found a place to live. The lack of medicine to keep his diabetes under control had been holding him back from living independently.

Marianne Haver Hill at MEND says that with $10,000 her organization could supply life-sustaining medicine for five months to those in need, a very large portion of whom are diabetic and unable to afford insulin, the most basic of medicines.

The Boys & Girls Club of the West Valley occupies a building in – to put it charitably (pun intended) – terrible condition. The roof needs repair and leaks rivers during rain, the entire building needs painting, and there is no air conditioning or heating.

Imagine how the young people who the Club is trying to help will stifle in this summer's heat just to enjoy the Club...which is here to keep them off the streets and out of trouble. Jan Sobel at the Boys & Girls Club says it would take $35,000 to air condition and heat her Canoga Park facility.

New Horizons' 800 or so clients, who contend with Down Syndrome, autism, and a variety of other developmental challenges, take their breaks and lunch in the organization's quad, which lacks appropriate facilities and accommodations.

The organization's Holly Rasey tells us that $20,000 would provide new tables, benches, and other enhancements to replace their current 30-year-old, worn-out ratty fiberglass outdoor furniture, none of which is wheelchair accessible.

Far be it from me to tell others how to spend their money, but...

According to the *San Fernando Valley Business Journal Book of Lists*, the following were the highest-paid public company CEOs in our area in 2005:

- Angelo Mozilo, Chairman/CEO of Countrywide Financial Corp., had an aggregate take-home pay of $141,975,000.

- R. Chad Dreier, Chairman, CEO and President of Ryland Group, Inc., had an aggregate take-home pay of $57,630,000.

- Number three on the list was Kevin W. Sharer, CEO and President of Amgen, Inc., with an aggregate take-home pay of $34,487,000.

Now, I don't question that all three of these gentlemen might personally be very philanthropic, that their companies operate at the highest standards of community support, and that they may direct their firms to support the most deserving social agencies in their communities, to the greatest possible degree.

But I'd still bet that they can afford just a bit more philanthropy.

Mr. Mozillo, how about providing the air conditioning and heating for the Boys & Girls Club?

Mr. Dreier, how about some new furniture for New Horizons' clients?

Mr. Shearer, how about five months' worth of medicines for MEND's beneficiaries?

Gentlemen, it's up to you whether your tax-deductible contributions come from your organizations or each of you, personally. But let's help these organizations now, not after six months of corporate bureaucracy.

***

Charity begins at home.
—Charles Dickens

It's True: The Times They are A-Changin'

Bob Dylan's first album of all original music, released in 1964, got it right: the times they *are* a-changin'.

He knew it then, and we know it now: nothing is as it used to be...

It used to be easy to tell who was who in the old Western movies: the good guys wore white hats and the bad guys donned black ones (except for Hopalong Cassidy, who was definitely a good guy, but wore a black hat).

Today, no one wears a hat...of any color. The old labels are dying out...kinda.

It used to be that if you were a Democrat, all Republicans were right-wing nuts; if you were a Republican, all Democrats were left-wing nuts. Our elected officials could always be counted on to be what they were...but no longer.

On one hand, for example, City Council President Eric Garcetti received well-deserved kudos, in concert with other Council members, for leading the fight for business tax reform (a job not yet completed); then he turns around and sends an ill-conceived letter warning potential conventioneers not to patronize the Airport

Hilton because the hotel doesn't pay its employees as *he* thinks they should.

It used to be that if you were a businessperson, labor was out to channel any meager company profits into the union's coffers; if you were a union member, business was out to grind the working man into abject poverty. And while labor and business still snarl at each other like contentious bulldogs, there have been a few glimmerings of cooperation, particularly when businesses really are in danger of failing...our airlines a few years ago and our auto industry more recently.

As the Valley keeps evolving, it becomes more and more difficult to deny change.

Just a few years ago, people would sneer at the mention of the Chatsworth-based adult film industry (we used to call them pornos). Today we think of it as an economic benefit and job source.

Cruising Van Nuys Boulevard was a long-standing Valley tradition. Our love affair with the automobile was a thing of beauty. But it's a love affair that's gone sour.

Unnecessary driving pollutes the atmosphere, adds to freeway congestion, and costs more than $3 a gallon. We've gone from muscle cars to miniscule cars. Sadly, the Dodge Charger 500 with a 426-cubic-inch Hemi engine is out and the Prius or some other fuel-efficient but stylistically challenged vehicle is in.

It used to be that if you lived or worked in Our Valley, you were a WASP, with a couple of Catholics and Jews thrown in just to spice up the mixture. But like everything else about the San Fernando Valley, its mix of ethnic and national communities has changed dramatically. According to the last census, fully 40 percent of Valley dwellers are foreign born. Today, Our Valley's 1.8 million residents represent the most diverse region of the city...and perhaps the nation.

The changes we're going through are scary for some. But we're fresh out of orange trees in the Valley, they're not filming Westerns at the RKO Studio Ranch, and bored housewives aren't hanging out in the afternoons at the Fireside Inn in Encino any more.

More than just a great writer, Isaac Asimov was a great thinker and futurist. He wrote: "It is change, continuing change, inevitable change, that is the dominant factor in society today. No sensible decision can be made any longer without taking into account not only the world as it is but the world as it will be. This, in turn, means that our statesmen, our businessmen, our every man must take on a science fictional way of thinking."

Our businesses will be as successful if they recognize and embrace change. There's no use lamenting for long-gone orchards or shuttered restaurants. Like it or not, we must enthusiastically embrace new technologies, new workforce demands, new societal imperatives, and new challenges from abroad.

Instead of denying the existence of greenhouse gases, let us be in the forefront of finding solutions. Instead of decrying the anti-business bent of our City Council, let us work to elect more pro-business representatives. Instead of seceding from Los Angeles, let us be sure we get our fair share of city services. Instead of complaining about offshore call centers stealing our jobs, let us create new kinds of jobs.

The old ways don't seem to work anymore. And maybe that's a good thing.

**

When you're finished changing, you're finished.
—Benjamin Franklin

Valley Business: Diversity at Work

Business in the Valley isn't just where – or what – we think it is.

A horseback survey (that means I asked four friends) shows that most of us think of the Valley business community as a barbell-shaped entity...two large round weights at Universal City and Warner Center, connected by a bar known as Ventura Boulevard.

If you're in need of a lawyer, an accountant, or a medical professional, there's probably some truth to that view. But the richness of Our Valley is that a kaleidoscope of businesses survive and thrive across our North-of-Mulholland region, and most of the people who work in them don't take elevators up several floors to oak-paneled offices.

Those of us who do work in offices know the truth of poet Robert Frost's view: "The brain is a wonderful organ; it starts working the moment you get up in the morning and does not stop until you get into the office."

Much of the best "work" in the Valley doesn't take place in offices...

Bobrick Washroom Equipment is one of the few remaining Valley-based companies founded more than a century ago.

In 1906, George Augustus Bobrick, a manufacturer of waxes and ammonias, conceived the idea of the first liquid soap dispenser and obtained a patent for it in 1908. He later developed a soap dispenser for Pullman railway passenger cars...and a soap dispensing giant was born.

The company has since morphed into the world's leading designer and manufacturer of washroom equipment and supplies, and celebrated its sixtieth anniversary in 1966 by moving into its new 32,000-square-foot headquarters building on Hart Street in North Hollywood...where the firm continues to be flush with success.

In May, 2005, then-Mayor Hahn selected Bobrick's North Hollywood headquarters as the location for signing Los Angeles' business tax reform ordinance.

And just when we feared the Valley would be taken over by an endless string of chain restaurants, hotels, and coffee shops...we stumble upon thriving businesses based on individuality and craftsmanship.

Take Silver King.

Designers of almost everything in silver you could imagine, Silver King was founded in 1977 by a couple who immigrated from Mexico, Miguel and Maria Davalos. Silver King is one of the many small shops located along Devonshire Street in Chatsworth, where the Old West still echoes.

Three of their four children, Marcia, Malila, and Miguel Jr., have turned the silversmith shop into a family affair, with Miguel Jr. now creating the new artistic designs.

Among their more fascinating creations is a belt buckle they made for Governor Arnold Schwarzenegger. Not to be outdone, Antonio Villaraigosa had the Davalos family create a buckle for him, which modestly proclaims in raised silver letters: "Los Angeles Mayor." Other celebrities who have found their way to the unprepossessing north-end-of-the-Valley shop are Tom Selleck, Dwight Yoakam, and Jennifer Tilly.

Miguel Jr. will be demonstrating the age-old art of silversmithing at the upcoming free SummerFest 2007, being held at the historic Chatsworth Train Depot on June 9.

And since we're at the north end of Our Valley...

When you think of Ted Diggins, only one word comes to mind: "grizzled." A wiry man who won't see sixty again, Diggins is one of the Valley's last farriers, or "horseshoer," to city slickers like me (and probably you).

Raised in West Virginia, Diggins grew up with horses. He started shoeing horses at 14 and has spent his whole life around them...except for the years he served in the military in Japan, Korea and Vietnam.

Diggins has been shoeing horses for more than 45 years, and has been living – and shoeing – in Chatsworth for 32 of them. He says he loves this area for its spirituality and its connection with the Native American cultures. He talks about standing on Devonshire Street and looking up at Pregnant Indian Mountain, and thinking about those who lived in this region hundreds of years ago.

Diggins reflects on his many years as a Man of the West: "I live every day as an adventure; the key things for success in my business are integrity, knowledge, and a sense of caring for horses. Every horse I shoe, I shoe as if it's my own horse," he says.

I love having my own business," Diggins says. "I'm the Employee of the Month every month."

"Diversity" has become one of the top ten politically correct words that pepper our 21st century nomenclature. Perhaps we should keep in mind that diversity is not just a word that refers to ethnic, racial, and religious groups, but to where we live and work... and what we do...as well.

Our Valley contains slightly more than 50,000 businesses, with a workforce of 825,000 people. And it includes people who make bathroom supplies, etch silver, and shoe horses.

Ain't that grand?

**

> *There's no labor a man can do that's undignified, if he does it right.*
> —Bill Cosby

A Classless Society with No Class

Last week I was called a curmudgeon.

It's probably true.

My good friend from England, Alan Capper, who now lives in and loves New York, says that the best thing about America is that people here succeed in business based on their abilities and other attributes, while in the U.K., success is still based on one's class. He calls it our American meritocracy.

He's probably right, but I'm afraid we've created a classless society...with no class.

While words like "style," "class," "elegance," and, yes, even "panache," are open to personal interpretation, they seem to have a decreasing importance to most of us.

In our frantic rush to multi-task our way through life, our decreasing concern for the feelings of others, and our win-at-any-cost approach to business and personal matters, we have nearly lost sight of what used to be called "the niceties of life."

Driving around Our Valley may be the most obvious example. It will come as no revelation that we all believe that drivers are less considerate of each other.

A Classless Society with No Class

Obviously, Detroit (remember when "Detroit" used to mean the entire auto industry?) doesn't provide directional signals any more. They are so rarely employed they must be an expensive option on most cars.

Stop signs are merely suggestions.

Changing lanes is a game of "chicken."

Heading east on the Ventura Freeway toward either Hollywood or Pasadena, one better get in the correct lane by Laurel Canyon Boulevard, because it's a rare driver who will open up space from the car ahead to let you into one of the two left lanes if you're headed toward the San Gabriel Valley.

Being the old-fashioned person I am, I once opened the door of my car for a female business associate with whom I was driving to a meeting.

"You don't have to open the door for me; I'm not broken," she commented just a bit haughtily.

"I didn't open the door for you because I thought you were broken, I opened the door for you because I thought you were a lady," I quickly and cleverly – and rudely – responded. I guess on that occasion neither of us showed much class.

And of course, the Fickle Finger of Fate used to refer to a skit on the old television show, *Laugh-In*. Now it's changed from the index finger to the middle finger.

So, as a public service, I have decided to provide a six-question self-administered quiz to help each reader of the *Business Journal* determine how much class he or she actually has. Here goes...

Do you write thank you notes on appropriate occasions?
- Never – no points
- Occasionally – 1
- Frequently – 2

How do you send thank you notes?
- Email – 1
- Typed – 2
- Handwritten – 3

When dining at Brandywine or Pinot Bistro, do you wear (using men's clothing as a gauge)?
- Jeans and a T-shirt – 0
- Slacks and a jacket/open-neck shirt – 1
- Tie and jacket – 2

When you've been asked to RSVP on an invitation to a business or social event, do you usually?
- RSVP "yes" but if something better comes along, don't show up, or call – 0
- Don't RSVP but show up – 0
- RSVP but show up late – 1
- RSVP and arrive on time – 3

In most business meetings, do you?
- Text message or read emails – 0
- Talk too much – 1
- Interrupt others – 1
- Feel that you have to say something about every topic – 1

What do you do with your cell phone during a business meeting?
- Leave it on ring and take a long call – 0
- Set it on silent/vibrate – 1
- Turn it off – 2

Instructions: add up your points...and decide how much class you have.

In 2003, Pepperdine's Graziadio Business School Journal interviewed Bert Boeckmann, and quoted him as saying:

"The people I have known who are really successful in the true meaning of the word have always tended to fit into the mold of honesty and integrity that we would call ethics today. Their basic integrity is not just measured in dollars, but is measured by their families, their friends, and their whole lives."

The next time you're in a business or social situation with Bert or Jane Boeckmann watch how they treat other people... with unfailing courtesy and respect. Those are people with class.

Then watch how some people chairing a meeting use their positions to sprinkle snide or even near-rude comments among those whose points of view they don't share. Those are not people with class.

Maybe more of us need to go to the head of the class.

***

> *What is lacking here is charm and taste.*
> —Frédéric-Auguste Bartholdi
> French designer/sculptor
> (referring to the U.S.)

There's No Sense at the Census

Once again, the Valley is being short-changed.

But this time, it's not the Over-the-Hill Gang in City Hall; it's some bureaucrats in our nation's Capital. Mr. Kincannon giveth...and Mr. Kincannon taketh away.

Seems that Director of the U.S. Census Bureau, Charles Kincannon, and his numbers-crunching minions have threatened to take away the Valley's separate census designation, something that VICA, the Economic Alliance, and others had been fighting for half a decade, and was just granted two years ago.

Now, normally census figures, statistics, and reports are not high on my list of priorities. In fact, they're just about at the bottom. My eyes tend to glaze over at columns of numbers, charts, and graphs. But any potential slight to Our Valley's individuality raises my hackles (wherever *they* are).

Recently, the Census Bureau floated a proposal to rescind the nationwide designation that established us as a distinct demographic area. It's all kind of technical, but important enough to try to understand.

There's a whole section in the Census Bureau's categories, created fifty years ago, called Census County Divisions (CCDs), the statistical identification under which Our Valley is designated as a specific place. Two years ago, they let us in (guess we weren't a specific place until then).

But Mr. Kincannon *et al.* are saying those categories aren't used much, based on visits to their website, so they're thinking of doing away with them.

Of course, Our Valley would be only the sixth-largest city in the nation were it not for the hardball tactics of Mayor Jimmy, located in the country's most important state (nothing personal, Idaho), so why should statistical information about us be important?

It's simple. A quick review of the recently published San Fernando Valley Economic Research Center's report shows that the Valley is clearly a different demographic from the rest of the city: more diversity, less unemployment (or, if you want to put it in the positive, more employment), higher per capita income, etc.

Data is not just a character on *Star Trek*; it's the distillation of who – and what – we are, and a gauge of what we can become.

Now, don't you think our realtors who are seeking to bring residents and businesses here find that a compelling picture of a region is helpful to them? Don't you think those considering relocating their businesses here care about our colleges and universities and our well-educated workforce?

Don't you think not-for-profits across the Valley who are applying for government aid to assist their community-benefiting programs have a better chance of obtaining it if they can present a clearer picture of the area they serve?

Don't you think we stand a better chance of our fair share if we define ourselves as what we are...part of the city...yet distinct from it?

Don't you think marketers feel they can do a better job of reaching their clients and customers if they have more information about them?

It's not just a numbers game, Mr. Kincannon.

As one elected official put it in his letter to the head of the Census Bureau: "The San Fernando Valley is a unique area, facing a different set of challenges, and requiring a different set of solutions than the rest of the City of Los Angeles."

Somehow it feels that if we lose our hard-won separate designation we'll be the regional equivalent of a Soviet-era non-person. At least in the eyes of demographers (I've always wanted an opportunity to use that word) our North-of-Mulholland community will be lumped in with that South-of-Mulholland world.

Besides, think how much harder Dan Blake's job at CSUN would be without these numbers.

***

> *There are lies, damned lies, and statistics.*
> —Benjamin Disraeli
> English Prime Minister

Leaving California for Nebraska?

I started to write about the missing-in-action state budget.

How the inability of California's State Senators to agree on how to effectively spend the money we give them is on the verge of creating major problems for many segments of society.

How childcare centers, some 11,000 nursing homes, facilities for the developmentally disabled, and many other Medi-Cal-funded institutions just aren't being paid...and are having a tough time paying their employees and other bills.

How funding for community colleges and Cal Grants to students are held up by the Senate's 25 Democrats and 15 Republicans.

Of course, how we've managed to create such a dysfunctional legislative system is beyond the understanding of most of us. California joins Arkansas and Rhode Island as the only three states in the Union that require a two-thirds vote in both houses of their legislatures to approve a budget.

So while our Sacramento solons fiddle, the world's sixth-largest economy is brought to a standstill. Healthcare issues; highway and other infrastructure repairs; water issues; and just a few other such unimportant matters lie unattended to so that legislators can blame "special interests," each other, and anyone but themselves, for the current situation.

If you log onto the State Senate website (www.senate.ca.gov), and go to the page of schedules, you'll be informed that a month-long "summer recess" begins on July 20, "provided (the) budget bill has been passed." No budget bill has been passed, but try to find any of our Senators in the Capitol.

Comedienne Lily Tomlin might have been speaking of our Sacramento leaders when she said, "Ninety-eight percent of the adults in this country are decent, hardworking, honest Americans. It's the other lousy two percent that get all the publicity. But then, we elected them."

The Economist magazine says of California's budget-setting impasse that "the legislature was debating a budget that one senator described as having been written by chimpanzees." The truth is, they're making monkeys out of themselves...and, yes, we get no bananas.

But I decided not to write about the budget impasse... it's too depressing.

Instead, I considered moving to Nebraska.

Why Nebraska?

It's the only state in the nation with a unicameral legislature...meaning one house. And to make it even better, Nebraska's 49 legislators are elected on a nonpartisan basis. Senators are elected to four-year terms and receive a salary of $12,000 a year. The state is divided into 49 legislative districts, each containing approximately 35,000 people. (By comparison, California's Senators each represent 846,791 people in one of the most gerrymandered states in the nation.)

In Nebraska, a candidate's political party is not listed on the election ballot. The two candidates who obtain the most votes in the primary election face each other in the general election. So, unlike our Fair California, Nebraska's legislative leadership is not based on party affiliation.

A new experiment in governance? Not exactly; Nebraska has had a single legislative house since 1937. And they're very happy with it, those Cornhuskers.

What would such a system mean in California? No party bosses or group voting; no expenses for 80 Assembly members and 40 Senators for a total of 120 elected officials, their staffs and their expenses; and no wrangling over minor language in bills in committees representing the two legislative houses.

The truth is, whether we adopt something similar to Nebraska's 70-year-old approach to the legislative branch, keep what we have, or simply blow up the system, there's an old saw that's operative here: People get the government they deserve.

Until we have the political will to really teach our elected officials, at all levels of government, that they work for us, we don't work for them; until we find a way to let them know that their focus on scoring political points works to the detriment of the people and is unacceptable; and until we find our way out of this quagmire of partisan bickering, our state and our nation will continue to flounder.

Of course, Nebraska doesn't have Paris Hilton, Britney Spears, or girlie boys. Maybe I'll stay here after all. How bad could it really be?

***

> *Laws are like sausages, it is better not to see them being made.*
> —Otto von Bismarck
> First Chancellor of Germany

Valley Fights Whites-Only Image

If we have to have gangs – and would that we didn't – isn't it comforting to know that we have white gangs, black gangs, Latino gangs, Asian gangs, and Armenian gangs? We're so diverse!

I don't know if Our Valley can boast Samoan gangs, Jewish gangs, or Canadian gangs, but it would not be surprising to learn that we did.

Just in the last two weeks, I've seen signs in the Valley in Spanish (Pacoima), Hebrew (Encino), Thai (Van Nuys), Russian (Tarzana), Farsi (North Hollywood), Armenian (Glendale), and a few that I couldn't tell you what language they were in.

And yet the Valley's reputation as a bastion of "white flight" continues to persist in films, literature, and popular culture.

But that which was once true is not necessarily true today.

There's no denying that much of Our Valley's post-World-War-II growth is based on Anglos fleeing the city's homogenizing core; that the proliferation of private schools and the anti-school-busing movement was more about race than education; and that many Valley real estate covenants contained clauses such as: "No one whose blood is not entirely of the

Caucasian race will be permitted to own property in this subdivision."

That effectively kept out those whose skin color was black, brown, or yellow.

The most recent demographic figures show what a melting pot the Valley has become. Of the 1,742,760 of us, 61 percent are Caucasian, 41 percent Latino, 11 percent Asian, and four percent African American. Many of us are part of more than one group, accounting for a total above 100 percent.

But our "Whites Only" history, although long a thing of the past, persists in the minds, and pens, of out-of-touch writers.

Just a few years ago, for example, John Patterson, editorializing in the highly respected English newspaper, *The Guardian*, wrote, with more than a touch of that vaunted British snobbishness:

"The Valley...(is) acquiring its share of intoxicated residents... eager to proselytize (sic) on its behalf, to hymn its lily-white weirdness, and mine its rich seams of inch-deep history and suburban surrealism... The catalogue of differences extends to the Valley's beleaguered suburban homesteader mindset, its near-Iowan racial homogeneity, and even its climate...If [a successful secession movement occurred] the resulting metropolis would be the nation's seventh largest, and by some considerable measure its whitest."

John, you're a generation or two out of date.

But just to demonstrate how pervasive the outdated "white flight" to the Valley image is even today, this is a snippet from CBS's Katie Couric's May 11, 2007, online interview with urbanist Joel Kotkin.

Katie asks: "...How is Antonio Villaraigosa doing in a city that has long seen tension between its rising Latino population, its significant African American minority, and 'white flight' toward the San Fernando Valley and away from the city center?"

Joel responds: "The Valley is not losing whites as fast as before, I believe, but cannot be sure. Many areas are becoming attractive to middle class of all ethnicities, including in particular Persians, Armenians, and Asians, but also many entertainment industry people."

In other words, Katie still thinks that there's "white flight" **to** the Valley, while Joel talks about "white flight" **from** the Valley.

Katie, get with the program.

The truth is, the Valley as a whole has become home to people from every corner (how can a round planet have corners?) of the globe, yet they tend to congregate with others of similar backgrounds.

People have been living with others like themselves from the beginning of society. They grapple with some of the same issues, enjoy the same foods, laugh at the same jokes...in essence, we all feel most comfortable with others with whom we share something in common.

In Boston, the Italians and Irish staked out their own neighborhoods; in Chicago, there are sharp demarcations between various nationalities' residential areas; and the Valley is no different.

There's nothing wrong with people choosing to live with others of their racial, national or ethnic background...as long as they do so because they want to, not because they have to.

∗∗∗

If man is to survive, he will have learned to take a delight in the essential differences between men and between cultures. He will learn that differences in ideas and attitudes are a delight, part of life's exciting variety, not something to fear.
—Gene Roddenberry
Creator of Star Trek

Sub-Par Thinking On Sub-Prime Loans

The innumerable "whooshing" sounds you hear are not the near-silent falling of a house of cards.

They are the falling of cards of houses...or, to be more precise, the millions of pieces of paper upon which sub-prime mortgages are written.

And falling with them is the rest of the economy.

So what are these papers that can bring our economy to its collective knees? They are loans provided to people who couldn't afford to repay them, sold by people who should have known better than to make them. And then, to compound the problem, millions of these loans were packaged as "financial investments" by the firms employing those high-flying youngsters working for such Wall Street investment houses as Bear Stearns.

And leave it to those geniuses to create a phrase, "sub-prime mortgages." Why not a bit more truth in packaging: "loans to those who can't afford them sold by those who don't care."

Isn't that much more descriptive?

We Americans love to place blame, so let's decide who's to blame here.

Is it the borrowers who found a way to purchase property that they hoped they'd be able to afford when their adjustable rate mortgages were reset – at a higher rate, of course? Well, maybe in some cases, but who can blame ever-optimistic Americans who are sure they'll be making more in three years than they are today.

Sadly, when it comes to borrowing – and a mortgage is a loan – they disregarded the old saw that "if it sounds too good to be true, it probably is."

Should we wag our collective fingers (no, not the middle one) at the companies that created and sold these loans? Are these companies just rapacious predators out to take advantage of poor, misguided individuals longing for their share of the American dream? Probably to some degree, but in a capitalistic society, the concept is to sell something for more than it costs.

And finally, there are the twenty-somethings on Wall Street, whom we all secretly despise for making millions not too much after they began shaving regularly, while the rest of us poor working stiffs toil away for a mere few thousands a year.

In their usual well-thought-out and results-oriented approach to the problem, our lawmakers, from the U.S. Capitol in Washington to Los Angeles City Hall, figure the best way to solve the problem is to throw money at it...our money, of course.

Having previously assumed the mantle of the Old Curmudgeon, it pains us not one bit to suggest that those who made bad decisions about managing their money have to be responsible for those decisions, and that those businesses that sold mortgages they knew couldn't be paid back choke on their own loan papers.

Every pundit, prognosticator, and politician seems to have a magical solution to the problem. The truth is, there isn't one. Our economy is going to have to go through a year or so of too many unsold houses on the market, too many people suffering from the burden of repaying loans they can't afford, and too many ripples going through the rest of our Iraq-war-burdened economy.

There, doesn't that cheer up your Monday morning?

Here in Our Valley, we're definitely feeling the fallout: real estate agents are scurrying for viable listings, homebuilders are trying to reduce inventory, and jobs are being lost in every sector of the economy.

Nestled in the hills of Calabasas is the mortgage industry giant, Countrywide Financial. Their website's home page reads: "As the #1 home loan lender in the country, we specialize in finding ways to say 'yes!'" Maybe it should be changed to: "As the #1 home loan lender in the country, we specialize in finding ways to say "'yes – when it makes sense!'"

The company is laying off thousands of employees, suffering from negative press over its recalcitrance to work with struggling homeowners looking for some assistance, and casting about for additional cash infusions to remain viable.

According to its third-quarter financial results, things are pretty scary at Countrywide Financial: "Mortgage loan fundings for the month of September 2007 totaled

$21 billion, a 44 percent decline from September 2006...Average daily mortgage loan application activity for September 2007 was $1.7 billion, a 39 percent decrease from September 2006."

One person not struggling too much in all of this is Countrywide's Chairman/CEO, Angelo Mozilo, who according to the *San Fernando Valley Business Journal*, had an aggregate take-home pay of $141,975,000 in 2005.

Back in March, we suggested to Mr. Mozilo that he and a few other extremely well-compensated (that's corporate-speak for "what an outrageous salary"!) senior executives could help a few Valley philanthropies in dire short-term need, suggesting his organization of choice might be the Boys & Girls Club of the West Valley.

None of the three executives we mentioned chose to heed our suggestion.

Mr. Mozilo, maybe you need some positive PR now more than ever. The Boys & Girls Club raised the money for their heating and air conditioning, but they sure could use a van or two to transport needy kids to a safe environment like the Club.

Think about it.

***

There is no such thing as a free lunch.
—Robert Heinlein
Author

The Professor Tells it Like it Is

One of the things I like about Shirley Svorny is that she tells it as it is.

As Professor and Chair of CSUN's Department of Economics, Shirley pulled no punches when she addressed VICA's Business Forecast Conference earlier this month.

She spoke about the impact of less-than-optimum public policy on our economy...and, of course, Los Angeles' public policy is set by our Mayor, the 15 City Council members who pretty much run their own fiefdoms, and the bureaucrats who (too often) make policy by the manner in which they implement the policies set by those 16 elected officials.

How is this for honesty on the part of the Good Professor?: "In most cases, the strategies adopted by the city are poorly thought out and a waste of money."

She gave a number of examples of how the city telegraphs, not too subtly, its willingness to wield its public policy club to over-regulate business, including its prohibition on Wal-Mart Supercenters from locating in city limits; its 2005 law dictating rules of employment for large grocery stores; and the recent, albeit unsuccessful, attempt to require a living wage for employees of hotels located near LAX.

She feels that these actions have impacts way beyond the targeted industry; they give other businesses the impression that our City Council is capricious in its policy-setting – that it picks on specific businesses and industries whenever it wants to. Not a good message to send when you're in competition with a brace of surrounding cities that hang out a very large and well-lit welcome sign to disaffected Los Angeles businesses.

There's no secret to what Professor Svorny – and most other experts – think would go a long way toward dealing with the perception (and perception is reality) that we live in one of the nation's least business-friendly metropolises: "I'd lower business taxes and reform the difficult-to-navigate city bureaucracy that holds businesses up. But even simpler...the best thing local government can do to promote job creation and prosperity would be to focus on things we need from government... police actions to eliminate gangs; road repair; maintenance of the medians and other common property; and at the top of my list, I'd put improving the local public schools."

She points out that a key element of a city's economic strategy should be protection of its tax base. Using as an example Universal Studios' plan to develop its property, which is facing opposition from nearby residents, she makes an indisputable point: "If you don't let developers build new homes and commercial and industrial buildings, all you have are old homes and old commercial and industrial properties, which are less attractive to growing businesses and their employees.

"It's all well and good to want to maintain the ambiance of a neighborhood," she says, "but what are all the costs of doing that? Developers don't want to have to face long delays in development, costly legal challenges and opposition by neighbors. When we act this way, we might as well say, Don't come here and fix up our aging buildings and neighborhoods.' There is a real loss associated with these actions."

NIMBYism, anyone?

With tongue pressed firmly in cheek, Ye Olde Columnist asks if it's really possible that our city's high business tax rates; complicated regulatory requirements and its enforcing bureaucracy; and residents who stymie efforts for residential, industrial, and commercial development, might actually drive corporations and entrepreneurs away.

Some of our City Council members have begun to talk the talk; it remains to be seen if they'll walk the walk. The September 21 issue of the *Daily News*, in its page one lead article, reported on how the Mayor and the President of the Council said that they know that successful businesses are a cornerstone of a successful city.

Remember those colorful street pole banners that proclaimed "L.A.'s the Place"? I've always wondered how many businesses that were considering leaving for Burbank, Glendale, Pasadena, Santa Monica, Culver City, Calabasas, or Santa Clarita, remained in the City of the Angels because of those pole banners.

Professor Svorny points out that there are strong indications that new industries might grow and prosper here "if we were to reduce the business tax, facilitate business permitting, and streamline other government regulations. Who knows how many jobs and how much wealth would be created?"

Shirley for City Czar, anyone?

***

> *The government solution to a problem is usually as bad as the problem.*
> *—Milton Friedman*
> *Economist*

Tale of Kvelling in Canoga Park

It's not too often that one has the opportunity to *kvell* at the corner of Victory Boulevard and Canoga Avenue (Note to those linguistically challenged by Yiddish: it's pronounced in one syllable, not like the nurse, Edith Cavell.)

Kvelling is the feeling you get when your child steps up to receive his or her college diploma, when you hold your first grandchild, or when your loved one steps off a plane having safely returned from war in Iraq or Afghanistan.

It all started a few months ago.

In celebration of having operated my firm in the Valley for 25 years as of September 1, I decided to donate $25 to each of 25 youngsters at the Boys & Girls Club of the West Valley. The money was to be used for one purpose: each of them was to spend the money on books; not DVDs, not CDs, not video games...books.

The staff at the Boys & Girls Club put together a great literacy program, which is one of the Club's emphasis areas.

The staff created a program for the elementary school youngsters called "Book Worm." Each of the children read as many books as they could, according to their grade level. Upon completion of their book, they each filled out a book report and received a segment of the "book worm" that was put on a Club wall. Those who read the most books won the prize in each grade.

The middle and high school youngsters' program was based on writing a poem, with the staff judging the most creative.

Last week, about 21 of the 25 youngsters met me at the Borders book store in Canoga Park, each of them in their powder blue Boys & Girls Club t-shirts. Paul Hixenbaugh and Janette Caredda of the store's staff were on hand to help the children select their books.

Wasting no time, one youngster asked without hesitation, "Where are the books on wrestling?" and immediately charged up the stairs to the second floor sports section.

One little girl, about 10, came up to me, took my hand, looked up at me with her big brown eyes and said, "I don't know how to start; will you help me find a book?"

A particularly precocious young man of about 13 selected upwards of a dozen books, all adult reading level, on such subjects as the end of World War II and the Crusades, and put them in his overburdened black shopping bag. It pained him to have to return a few.

A little pony-tailed girl looked around the store and admitted, "I've never been in a book store before." I felt like a hero.

"I didn't know what I could get [afford] for my little brother; now I can get him a book for Christmas," admitted a slender little girl of about nine. I felt like a Jewish Santa Claus.

A teenager asked me to help her find a mystery book. I turned her on to Agatha Christie, telling her that the English author had written more mystery novels than anyone in history, and that she could make practically a lifetime of reading out of Miss Marple, Hercule Poirot, and Tommy and Tuppence Beresford.

The children's shopping bags were filled with books about dinosaurs, about Barbie dolls, about sports stars, about movie stars, about Thomas the Tank Engine...in fact, with just about everything you could imagine.

After they had all selected their books and they had been paid for, with the extra benefit of a much-appreciated discount from the store itself, the Boys & Girls Club staff posed them all up around me for a photograph. At the urging of Ed Crowe, our ace photographer for the afternoon, they all held up their filled Borders' bags and shouted in unison, "Thank you, Marty!"

That was by far the best holiday present I'll get this year.

As they filed out of the store and into their vans, I realized that I had learned a valuable lesson: writing a check to a charity or social agency is easy, becoming involved is what's satisfying.

This year, think about how you can *kvell*. It's not a feeling reserved for Jews, Christians, Muslims, Buddhists, or agnostics. It's reserved for all of us.

Find a way to get involved with people who deserve your support and assistance. If you do, you'll never go back to just writing a check in December for a tax deduction and forgetting about what the money is dedicated to achieving.

I know I won't.

✳✳✳

I cannot live without books.
—President Thomas Jefferson

Settling for Less than Utopia

They're rioting in Africa
There's strife in Iran
What nature doesn't do to us
Will be done by our fellow man.

Accurate as those lines are, they don't come from yesterday's *Daily News* or *Los Angeles Times*. They're from "The Merry Minuet," a Kingston Trio song recorded on their album, *From the Hungry I*...in 1959!

Yes, they are definitely rioting in Africa and there is certainly strife in Iran. And our fellow man does seem to be doing to us what nature doesn't.

A few examples:

- The NCAA, that paragon of rectitude, is investigating our own Encino resident, 97-year-old John Wooden for having dinner with a potential recruit (anyone not heard of UCLA's Kevin Love yet?) and his parents.

- Angelo Mozilo, that paragon of wreck, will walk away from Calabasas-based Countrywide Financial with a severance package in excess of $100 million, leaving strewn behind him the lives of 12,000 now out-of-work employees, including many from Our Valley.

- The Governor, that paragon of politics, has changed his mind, now supporting Speaker of the State Assembly Fabian Nunez' ballot measure that sounds like term limits reform, but in reality extends his own ability to stay in office.

We've begun 2008 with the same head-shaking illogical society with which we ended 2007.

Perhaps there's a parallel universe, and in that universe John Wooden is praised by the NCAA, Angelo Mozilo gives some of his millions to the needier among his fired employees, and the Governor doesn't offer a *quid pro quo* in return for support of his own agenda.

In my parallel universe, no LAPD officers would have to reveal their personal finances; major studios and networks would recognize the absolute necessity of writers and compensate them accordingly; gasoline would sell for a buck a gallon; and M.E.N.D. would go out of business because there would be no hungry or poorly clothed people left in the Valley who needed help.

Of course our transportation patterns would change in that parallel universe, as well:

- Reseda Boulevard would connect with Mulholland to alleviate street congestion through Reseda, Tarzana, Encino, and Sherman Oaks.

- Santa Clarita, Palmdale, Lancaster, and other cities whose growth forces traffic down the I-5 and 405 Freeways to jobs in our city would make amends by giving Los Angeles millions of dollars in reparations to improve traffic flow.

- And we'd finally figure out that you can have a city where jobs are close to residences, significantly reducing the time, cost, and stress of commuting.

Technology would play an important place in the parallel universe.

Cell phones would be programmed to automatically self-destruct if utilized in an automobile with its engine running. Drivers of SUVs and Hummers who park in spaces clearly marked "Compact Cars Only" would return to their vehicles to find them shrunk to fit within the spaces. *Star Trek*'s food replicators would do away with the necessity for cooking. Instead of Captain Picard's command, "Tea. Hot. Earl Gray," I could see myself ordering from my den chair, "Pastrami. On rye. Brent's Deli."

Government would change dramatically.

Our elected officials would not be able to vote themselves and each other raises while we suffer from deficits, struggle to avoid recession, and see escalating unemployment figures. There would be 20 or so Los Angeles County Supervisors, not five, bringing government closer to the governed.

Los Angeles City Council members and the Mayor would be mandated to provide a rolling strategic plan to address issues such as water, transportation, growth, and other such matters that are now addressed in a patchwork fashion. And of course, ill-advised, illogical, and ill-conceived business taxes would be eliminated.

Not that we're the first to hunger for the perfect society.

The 16th century English lawyer, author, and statesman, Sir Thomas More, coined the word "utopia" in his 1516 book. Utopia was the name he bestowed upon an idealized perfect society existing on an imaginary island.

We don't really need that utopia, but it would be nice to do away with the rioting in Africa and the strife in Iran. And the pain of families whose sons and daughters die in wars over the centuries and around the globe.

***

The saddest aspect of life right now is that science gathers knowledge faster than society gathers wisdom.
—Isaac Asimov
Author and futurist

When my computer is down I turn to my trusty 1917 Imperial Model B, with its curved keyboard. It's totally reliable, consumes no electricity, and is a lot more attractive than a computer. It *is* difficult finding good ribbons and carbon paper, though.

In Praise of the Type Cast Machine

Consider the typewriter. Yes, the lowly, bulky, near-extinct typewriter.

"Computers have changed the world," I've heard more than one person opine. No argument, but I'm here to defend the typewriter as having had just as great an impact on our business world as the computer has had.

It's not an implement in today's office anymore, unless your assistant uses one for odd-sized documents. ("Assistant" is the PC word for secretary, which is a perfectly honorable profession whose description should not have been thrown on the trash heap of political correctness.)

I collect typewriters...so far, about 40 of them. Some in my household would prefer I collect stamps or post cards with pretty pictures of long-gone tourist attractions. There are lots of antique typewriter collectors, but I don't know of any computer collectors. And for good reason.

Typewriters don't break down; I have some more than a century old that still work perfectly.

Typewriters don't support a legion of technicians who are half your age and three times as technologically savvy.

Typewriters don't freeze, give you a notice that "Your Underwood has a fatal flaw and must shut down," or flash warning lights that have absolutely no meaning to you.

Typewriters don't connect to a far-from-perfected Internet technology, printers that jam, or machines with names like "Linksys" or other arcane items available only at Fry's.

Typewriters do not lead to swearing, excuses to the boss that you can't provide the report he wants because your computer is down, or go into "sleep mode."

Although there were numerous machines based on the mechanical reproducing of individual letters in the mid-nineteenth century, the Sholes & Glidden machine is considered to be the first real typewriter; it was produced by E. Remington & Sons, in 1874. Because Remington, a well-known gun manufacturer, had hired an engineer who previously worked for a sewing machine company, the first typewriter looked suspiciously like one, treadle and all.

That first typewriter even had the QWERTY keyboard that still graces every computer keyboard, even though it is not the most efficient. In fact, it was specifically designed so that typewriter operators could not type so fast as to jam the keys.

I have typewriters from Germany, Israel, Estonia, England, and Belgium.

I have an Oliver typewriter whose keys come down from the sides, a Franklin with a curved keyboard that must have required a contortionist's skill, a Smith Premier with 70 keys, and several from the 19th century that don't have any keys at all.

I don't mess around with just Remingtons, Royals, Olivettis, and Smith-Coronas. I have such esoteric machines as a Mignon, Frolio, Fox, Hall's, Erika, and a Triumph.

There is romance in the long-forgotten names of many of these mechanical marvels: American Flyer, New American, Bambino, Ideal, Imperial, Empire, Monarch (these last three from England, of course), and the fabled Blickensderfer.

The first Blickensderfer ("Blick," to its friends) was introduced at the Chicago World's Fair, in 1893. More than 60 years before the IBM Selectric, the first electric typewriter was offered for sale by Blickensderfer in 1902; it failed because not enough people had electricity in their offices or homes.

It was the typewriter that provided women the opportunity to enter the workforce. How far they've come, and we've come, thanks to the typewriter.

In the Victorian Age, documents were written and copied by young men sitting at high desks. Women were not allowed in the workplace, primarily because they were perceived as not "having a head for business," likely to cause a distraction to young men with raging hormones, and better off tending the home fires.

When the typewriter came along, it was believed that only a woman could be what was initially called a "typewritist." Women were allowed into the previously all-male bastion of business because – it was believed – their smaller fingertips would fit the keys better and they could type rapidly without jamming the keys at the printing point.

Perhaps, had it not been for the lowly typewriter, Marie Curie would not have invented radium and, in 1903, become the first woman to win a Nobel Prize; a host of women would not have become presidents and prime ministers; and countless women would not have risen to the top in corporations around the world.

There are some who argue – with some justification – that the glass ceiling still exists, but it's a lot more easily shattered now because women were invited into the world's workplaces…but only because they had nimble fingers.

It's no stretch to believe that without the typewriter women would never have been invited out of the house and into the workplace…and the Democrats would not be close to nominating one for President.

See, the typewriter *has* changed the world.

***

> *The sound of a typewriter clacking away is a sound I miss now that everyone is writing on computers that just go ticky tack.*
> —Andy Rooney
> *60 Minutes* Commentator

It's Tough to Do the Right Thing

Why do we have such a difficult time doing the right thing?

Take the Israelis and the Palestinians, for example. Everyone knows the final deal: Israel stops building settlements and abandons those currently in the West Bank; allows free passage between the West Bank and the Gaza Strip; cedes part of Jerusalem to the Palestinians; and puts the Holy Places in that city under UN aegis. The Palestinians foreswear violence; recognize Israel; and punish those who commit terrorism. Simple, isn't it?

The same inability to do the right thing exists in Sacramento.

As long as the extremes of both parties stake out intransigent positions, the legislative process grinds to a halt. California used to be, and probably still is, an ever-so-slightly-to-the-left-of-middle state. Now we find our legislators in thrall to the extremes of both political parties.

One Valley-based Assemblyman told me that he has to vote a certain way because his party's caucus would never support anything he would propose in the future if he didn't vote as he was told.

Wouldn't it be great to have Sacramento legislators who voted solely based on what was best for their constituents and for all the people of California? Who knows, they might even come up with a fair approach to redistricting (remember that one, promised to us by Fabian Nunez, et al.?), and to solving a budget deficit of monumental proportions, an educational system worthy of the most backward of Southern states (no names here), and an infrastructure and water problems approaching critical.

Closer to home, there are the denizens of City Hall – that 28-story building whose tower is composed of concrete made with sand from each of California's 58 counties mixed with water from our 21 Missions. Do we honestly think we have a City Council composed of people dedicated to doing the right thing? Or are they doing what will get them elected to their next position?

I know of one City Council member (good news: he's not from the Valley) who admitted that he had to vote a certain way on a key issue because he sits next to a Councilman who holds a strong position on that issue... not because he necessarily shares that opinion.

Here in the Valley, wouldn't it be productive to hold reasoned, rational, discussions regarding development projects, such as the five proposed projects that begin at NBC Universal and go west? Of course not. Most people don't bother to make themselves knowledgeable...they just have opinions based on... who knows what?

Perhaps Bill Cosby's line is operative here: "A word to the wise ain't necessary – it's the stupid ones that need the advice."

And then there's the recent Holy Cross Hospital brouhaha. Only a naïf would think that all those who weighed in so vociferously were only concerned with patient care.

But let us not just shine the light of scorn on institutions and elected officials.

What kind of citizens are we?

Look at our own Presidential race. We make negative comments about John McCain because of his age, Hillary Rodham Clinton because of her gender, and Barack Obama because of his race. Wouldn't it be nice if we could just focus on who would make the best President in these troubled times?

And how many of those who speak with the most vigor will not even bother to vote in November?

And why do property owners have so little regard for their neighborhoods that they create those out-of-scale mansions that overshadow the lot and the community? Drive south on Hayvenhurst Avenue in Encino and take a look at the new "mansion" at the corner of Adlon Road...11,500 square feet of monstrous (couldn't think of a nicer word) house on a lot that shouldn't hold more than a 4,000-square-foot home.

And why do people put up signs for garage sales and fail to take them down afterward?

And why do shoppers leave shopping carts in the street?

And when will Ralphs and Gelson's across the Valley really take a leadership position in getting people to bring their own cloth bags instead of helping add to landfill burdens with "paper or plastic?"

And finally, a question for those who put up signs on telephone and street poles advertising Christmas lights installation: Are your signs left over from last December, or are you getting an early start on Christmas 2008?

It's easier to ask questions than to provide answers.

***

> It is not fair to ask of others what you are not willing to do yourself.
> —Eleanor Roosevelt

There Really Is a Here, Here

Famed author Gertrude Stein wrote in her book, "Everybody's Autobiography," that when she returned to California on a lecture tour in the 1930s she expressed a desire to visit her childhood home in Oakland. She couldn't find the house, and wrote, "There is no there there."

Many (mostly so-called media mavens and Westside wonks) have thought she might just as well been writing about Our Valley.

There are those ill-informed few who still think of the San Fernando Valley as an endless collection of post-World-War II cracker box houses. 'Taint true. Our communities have as much personality as any others in the country... we're just better at not taking ourselves too seriously.

Johnny Carson's beautiful downtown Burbank wasn't a put-down, it was a wry grin in the mirror. When Bob Hope said, "You know what San Fernando Valley is? Cleveland with palm trees," he forgot to mention that Toluca Lake was his beloved home for decades...and decades...and decades.

Our yesterdays and todays blend into a seamless time progression that defies easy chronologic divisions.

In the past, you knew you lived or worked in the Valley when:

- There were towns named Fernangeles, Girard, Platt Ranch, Dundee, Monte Vista, Oat Hills, Zelzah, and Roscoe – now all long gone.

- You ate at Otto's Pink Pig, Mary's Lamb, Don Drysdale's Dugout, the King's Arms, Tail o' the Cock, Moongate, or Farrell's Ice Cream Parlor.

- The newspapers were all writing about the latest likely traffic enhancements for the Valley, including the Reseda Freeway, Laurel Canyon Freeway, Sunland Freeway, Whitnall Freeway, Malibu Expressway, and the Mulholland Expressway.

- Just a few of your favorite tourist and recreational attractions were: Bird Wonderland in Encino, Busch Gardens in Van Nuys, the San Fernando Valley Fair at Devonshire Downs, the Iceoplex in North Hills, and the RollerCade in North Hollywood.

- You listened to KGIL or Magic 94FM...the Valley's own radio stations.

- You listened to jazz at Donte's, danced to country music at The Palomino, or rocked out at Bob Eubanks' teen-age club, the Cinnamon Cinder, where he staged The Beatles' first West Coast press conference in 1964.

- All of your favorite movie stars lived in the Valley: Clark Gable, William Holden, John Wayne, Lucille Ball and Desi Arnaz, Robert Redford, W.C. Fields, Bing Crosby, Al Jolson, James Cagney, Barbara Stanwyck, and hundreds more.

- You watched (but couldn't yet smell) the Budweiser plant going up in Van Nuys, in 1953...55 years ago.

- You were a member of the Road Runners, Valley Vegas, Vandits, Lobos, Valley Hi-Los, and Igniters, or one of the Valley's other car clubs that cruised Van Nuys Boulevard on Wednesday nights.

Today, you know you live or work in the Valley when:

- "Over the hill" relates to South-of-Mulholland, not your age range.

- You know at least five neighborhood streets that help you avoid the 405/101 interchange.

- You wait more than 90 minutes to be seated at Maggiano's.

- At least two of your City Councilmen are also reserve cops.

- You don't know anyone who has flown in or out of Whiteman Airport.

- You can see business signs in English, Spanish, Armenian, Hebrew, and Chinese...all in the same block.

- You don't have a single radio or TV station devoted to your 1.8-million-population region.

- "Rapid transit" means a bus.

- There are more Starbucks than hospitals.

There Really Is a Here, Here

- There are more Starbucks than gas stations.

- There may be more Starbucks than people (OK, just a slight exaggeration).

- When you've driven 17.2 miles of Ventura Boulevard and traveled through six communities (Woodland Hills, Tarzana, Encino, Sherman Oaks, Studio City, and Universal City) and never known where one ended and the next began.

- You Google "San Fernando Valley" and get 194,000 listings.

- You know that El Cab is not Spanish for a taxi.

"Yesterday" began long before August 5, 1769, when the Spanish explorer Gaspar de Portola led his group of 64 men and 100 mules through the Sepulveda Pass. Yesterday more likely began with the first Native American settlements, hundreds of years before that.

"Today" is gas hitting $4 a gallon, mansionization, and a Performing Arts Center at CSUN. What is truly fascinating is to watch one morph into the other, in fits and starts, ups and downs, pluses and minuses, as we observe Our Changing Valley.

***

> *The historian is a prophet looking backward.*
> —Friedrich Von Schlegel
> German philosopher

As President of the City's Quality & Productivity Commission, I'm presenting former LAPD Chief of Police William Bratton an award for one of his department's projects.

"To Serve and Protect" – Us

To me, he's still Tommy.

To everyone else he's Homicide Detective Thomas Townsend.

To me, he's my tow-headed nephew sitting on the side of his bed practicing his guitar.

To everyone else, he's one of Los Angeles' Thin Blue Line...the line that separates the law-abiding from the lawless.

Earlier this month was National Police Week, and on May 29, the annual Z Awards are presented to police and other public servants in recognition of outstanding service to Our Valley. So it's particularly appropriate to take a minute and think about those men and women who wear the blue uniforms.

The first modern police force was created by Sir Robert (that's why they're called "Bobbies" in England) Peel in 1829. They wore blue uniforms with copper buttons... hence the nickname, "coppers."

Prior to then, vigilante justice and neighborhood-watch-type organizations passed for public safety. Although not popular initially, soon Londoners were crying for more police on the streets...not unlike our own situation, where the allocation of police resources has been an issue for those who feel our North-of-Mulholland community is short-changed when it comes to public safety.

Frankly, I don't worry about it too much; as far as I'm concerned, what we don't have in quantity we more than make up for in quality.

With Deputy Chiefs in charge of the Valley Division such as Mark Kroeker, Marty Pomeroy, Mike Bostic, and Ron Bergmann, all of whom have been friends, the Valley Division has enjoyed superior leadership.

Pomeroy – now retired out of state – and I used to sign our notes to each other "The Other Marty," as if we were the only two Martys in the Valley.

Our current Deputy Chief, Michel Moore, carries on that tradition of leadership.

According to him, "Year-to-date we are down in overall crime nearly seven percent (1,115 fewer serious felony crimes than last year). In violence, we are down in every category… Overall gang crime is also down 18 percent and gang-related homicides down more than 50 percent."

Backing up – and often freeing up – the regular officers in the Valley is a cadre of business and community leaders reserve officers, for a total of 1,910 police personnel.

Two of the most notable reserve officers are a pair of Our Valley's City Council members, Dennis Zine and Greig Smith. And while we don't agree with every Council vote they cast, no one can argue that they don't deserve our respect and appreciation for their law enforcement volunteerism.

Of course, the ambivalence we feel toward the police is understandable. There's nothing we appreciate more than seeing a black and white pull up when we're in trouble, and nothing we resent more than when one pulls us over after we've gone through a red light (I wonder how many times a day they hear, "But it was still orange, officer").

One day several years ago, not yet a detective, Tommy came in to have lunch with me.

Resplendent in blue uniform, nightstick, gun, and his other "cop paraphernalia," he went to the receptionist – who like everyone else on staff – had no idea I had a police officer as a relative. The receptionist, in a slightly tremulous voice, informed my secretary that a policeman wanted to see me. That information took but seconds to spread throughout the office...and all eyes were on me as I walked out to meet the waiting officer of the law.

Upon seeing me, that blond policeman gave me a big hug...and I heard one of the nearby staff members wonder out loud, "Why is that cop hugging our boss?"

At one point, Detective Townsend was in the not-too-enviable situation of having to extract a criminal suspect from a white supremacist bar. A bit more cautious – and prudent – than was Eddie Murphy in the film *48 Hours*, he decided that ingenuity was to be preferred over bravado. So instead of going inside, he called the bar on the phone without identifying himself and whispered to the manager, "This is Jimmy, the cops are going to raid the place in 10 or 15 minutes..." Like rats fleeing a sinking ship, the bikers scurried from the establishment, scattered, and Townsend followed, and then arrested, the suspect.

When he was about 12, I asked Tommy why he wanted to be a policeman – since he had recently announced that to be his career choice. "To put all the bad people in jail," he told me.

Just last week, we had lunch at Mezzomondo in Studio City, and I asked him why he wanted to be in law enforcement. "To get all the bad guys off the street," he said, without a moment's hesitation.

The same answer – a quarter century apart – and I'm sure he didn't even realize it.

Do me a personal favor, the next time you pull up beside a police car or a couple of motorcycle officers at a red light, smile or wave at them...that's the least we owe them.

***

> *My heroes are those who risk their lives every day to protect our world and make it a better place – police, firefighters and members of our armed forces.*
> —Sidney Sheldon
> Author

What's the Valley's Gross National Happiness?

Does the San Fernando Valley have anything to learn from the tiny nation of Bhutan?

A Himalayan kingdom nestled among India, Nepal, and Tibet, with China looming ominously over its geographic shoulder, the entire nation of Bhutan is home to fewer than 700,000 people…less than half the population of Our Valley.

Bhutan's official government website mentions that the nation has 145 doctors. There are more than that along Ventura Boulevard between Sepulveda and White Oak Boulevards.

Druk Air, the Royal Bhutan Airlines, operates two A319 aircraft, making it the smallest national carrier in the world. There are no recorded instances of major community unrest over nighttime noise.

Thimphu, population 98,676, is the world's only capital city without a single traffic signal. There are, therefore, no recorded instances of cars running red lights.

The five branches of the Bhutan military forces total 8,000 people…fewer than the Los Angeles Police Department.

Bhutan is the only nation in the world where you can't smoke in public...and it is illegal to sell tobacco products. It is also the only nation in the world where plastic bags are considered an environmental hazard and are therefore illegal. Assemblyman Lloyd Levine was unsuccessful in getting a similar law passed in Sacramento

The Bhutanese are probably among the poorest – yet the happiest – people on earth.

We in the Western world have, for decades, defined economic growth and success in terms of Gross National Product (GNP).

And yet, this country of Buddhist monks, snow, and near-unpronounceable names has created a replacement phrase and concept that are beginning to resonate around the world: Gross National Happiness (GNH).

King Jigme Singye Wanchuck ascended the throne of Bhutan in 1972, and at that time coined the phrase to symbolize his commitment to building an economy based on the country's culture and Buddhist spiritual values.

While conventional development measurements focus on economic growth as the ultimate objective, the concept of GNH is based on the belief that society advances when material and spiritual development complement and reinforce each other.

In one of his campaign speeches shortly before his assassination in 1968, Presidential candidate Bobby Kennedy lamented that the GNP also grows because of the sales of rifles and knives and "television programs which glorify violence in order to sell toys to our children ... (it) does not allow for the health of our children, the quality of their education, or the joy of their play."

In 2005, writing in *Resurgence*, England's respected environmental publication, Rajni Bakshi wrote, "The evolving concept of GNH could well be the most significant advancement in economic theory over the last 150 years...Today it is widely acknowledged that the human economy cannot keep growing at the cost of its habitat. Yet even after two decades of expanding environmental regulation we are still losing the race to save the planet. This is partly because production systems and consumption patterns are out of sync with the carrying capacity of the planet. The pressure for ever higher GNP is merely one manifestation of this."

The four pillars of GNH are the promotion of equitable and sustainable socioeconomic development, preservation and promotion of cultural values, conservation of the natural environment, and establishment of good governance.

Sounds pretty simple – and logical – doesn't it?

So what does all this have to do with us? Have we perhaps gotten the spiritual and material out of whack right here?

Well, maybe it's time we asked ourselves whether true prosperity is more trees or more cement? Is happiness enhanced computer capabilities, PDAs, and other devices whose sole purpose is to allow us to work harder and longer?

Many a businessperson has arched his eyebrows at the mention of the president of Homeowners of Encino, who many believe would like Encino to return to what it was half a century ago. But perhaps there *is* merit in scrutinizing more closely what and where and how we build.

And then there's the issue of good governance. We live in an era where elected officials do not serve and then return to civilian life; instead, they play political musical chairs, starting to think about the next office they'll run for before they're termed out of the one they have. And there's no need to dwell on their propensity for living the high life at the public trough (Fabian Nunez, anyone?).

How about that near-sacrosanct mantra of democracy: "One man, one vote?" When our nation began, that "one man" meant one white man who met certain property qualifications…it did not include a black man, a woman, or someone who owned no property.

While we've corrected many of those inequities, in our heavily gerrymandered state we're still very far from equitable elections.

A headline in the May/June issue of *The American* magazine summed it up well: "Americans have on average gotten much richer over the past several generations. But there has been no meaningful rise in the average level of happiness."

The French writer and philosopher Albert Camus might have been referring to GNH when he wrote, "What is happiness except the simple harmony between a man and the life he leads?"

What's the Valley's Gross National Happiness?

Maybe a little less focus on Gross National Product and a little more on Gross National Happiness would be good for all of us in Our Valley.

✲✲✲

> *We have no more right to consume happiness without producing it than to consume wealth without producing it.*
> —George Bernard Shaw

Barking at the Dog Days of Summer

Well, here we are in the dog days of summer.

According to the Book of Common Prayer, published in 1552, the "Dog Daies" run from July 6 through August 17.

Originally, the dog days were those when the Dog Star, Sirius, rose just before sunrise. The Greeks would sacrifice a brown dog at the beginning of that period to appease Sirius, believing that the Dog Star caused the hot, steamy weather.

That arbiter of all things dictionary, Noah Webster, defined the hottest and muggiest part of the year as: "The period between early July and early September when the hot sultry weather of summer usually occurs in the northern hemisphere," and "a period of stagnation or inactivity."

We can certainly call this a summer of stagnation and inactivity in and around Our Valley.

Our City Council is stagnating when it comes to the strategic plan they said they would create for Los Angeles (isn't that one of the deliverables we were promised if we voted to extend term limits – which we did?).

The summertime malaise is palpable in near-empty retail stores and malls, with shoppers hesitating to spend money during this period of economic uncertainty. ("Economic uncertainty" is a euphemism for that dreaded word "recession".) "Inactivity" is the perfect word to describe the restaurants around the Valley; no longer need to book Café Bizou or Pinot Bistro two weeks in advance.

And "stagnation" would be preferred to what is happening in the real estate field in the Valley today. One of the Valley's largest commercial office building owners reports that just a few months ago he had more than 40 mortgage brokerage firms renting space in his buildings; now he's down to fewer than ten.

Of course, there are exceptions that prove the rule. If there is one thing that is not stagnating it's gasoline prices. No one has to be reminded that gas prices are well on their way to $5 a gallon. And remember our President's response, "I hadn't heard about that," when a reporter asked him about rumors of $4-a-gallon gas.

And it's not even worth a thimbleful of newsprint to write about the residential real estate market in the Valley. (At this point, there is a near-irresistible desire to write again about Angelo Mozilo and Countrywide Financial, but over salsa and chips at Sol Y Luna in Tarzana Ye Olde Editor suggested softly that I had been picking on poor Mr. Mozilo enough).

It would be nice to be able to look to our elected leaders to pull us out of the political, economic and governance morass in which we find ourselves, but there's probably little hope for that.

Our state's budgetary process is an embarrassment. The Pew Center on the States gives California a D+ for fiscal management... tied for dead last with Rhode Island. It doesn't get much worse than that. Almost every state began a new budget year the first of July... California is just one of four states in the nation without an approved budget by that date.

Partisanship in Sacramento is so rampant that there is little chance to see our legislators come up with real solutions to our very real problems. For some reason, my suggestion of locking the restrooms in the Capitol building until a state budget is signed, a redistricting process is in place, and term limits are revised, has met with little support.

And many of our city, county, and state officials act as if they have never heard of the concept of not only being above reproach, but appearing to be above reproach; we call it the Caesar's Wife Syndrome.

Pompeia, Julius Caesar's second wife, was implicated in a scandal in 61 BC stemming from the annual Feast of the Great Goddess. Though men were not admitted to this ritual, a well-known scalawag of the time, Publius Clodius, allegedly disguised himself as a woman and seduced her. Caesar immediately divorced Pompeia and an inquiry was held. The court asked Caesar why he had demanded a divorce when so much uncertainty surrounded the incident.

"Caesar's wife," he replied, "must be above suspicion."

Do our elected officials act as if they should expect to be above suspicion? Giving a $100,000 bonus to a staffer for campaign consulting work, buying thousands of dollars of wine with public money for fellow junketers, taking money donated to a campaign and using it for personal purposes...these are realities, as they say, ripped from today's headlines.

Perhaps most surprising of all, elected officials in feigned wonderment express surprise that we don't trust them.

So, let's summarize: the economy's in the toilet, our leaders can't agree on what to do, and we don't trust them anyway. The dog days of summer are a bitch.

***

Do the right thing. It will gratify some people and astonish the rest.
—Mark Twain

Turning the Page on the Los Angeles Times

OK, the fat lady has sung, the straw has broken the camel's back, the well has run dry, and it's all over but the shouting. I'm officially over the *Los Angeles Times*...

We've had a mutually satisfying affair for more than 40 years: I've sent them money; they've dutifully delivered my morning paper.

I've laughed with Jim Murray, dug jazz with Leonard Feather, railed at City Hall with Bill Boyarsky, chuckled at Conrad's cartoons, followed motor racing with Shav Glick, and listened to pop sounds with Robert Hilburn.

In the dim past of my youth I drew a paycheck from the Old Lady of Spring Street, downed a couple of beers with columnist Art Ryon at the Red Log, and hung out in the pressroom. I remember a newsroom littered with crumpled up sheets of paper with half-written stories on them that just weren't good enough, desks with manual typewriters, and pneumatic tubes rushing copy from one department to another.

I can still work a linotype machine, remember the California Job Case, and know how to set type in a stick.

But most of all, I remember that the people who put out the paper knew they were doing something important. They were aware they weren't just working for a business; they were the public's watchdog, the purveyor of what was happening around the world, the translator of the complexities and excesses of government.

First published as the *Los Angeles Daily Times* on December 4, 1881, *The Times* became a dominant figure in not only the history of Los Angeles, but also of the state. After 119 years of bombings, strikes, water wars, world wars, and a century of reporting news, the Times-Mirror Company was purchased by the Tribune Company of Chicago in 2000; that, as they say, was the beginning of the end.

Then came new technologies, diminished circulation and advertising revenues, and a parade of publishers and editors trying to plug holes in the sinking ship. And then Sam Zell arrived on the scene, an out-of-towner who bought the paper on April 2, 2007…just one day after April Fool's Day.

The following week, the *Times* Book Review became part of the Opinion section.

I've remained loyal through the axing of the Garfield cartoon strip, the shifting and eliminating of sections, the mass layoffs of first-rate journalists, and the basic emasculation of what once was a newspaper of which we could be proud. I reluctantly acquiesced when they combined the Opinion and Book Review sections back-to-back.

But now they've gone too far.

They're doing away with the separate Book Review Section.

The July 21 edition of *Publisher's Weekly* reported: "the *Los Angeles Times* is folding its standalone Sunday book review section, [and] laying off two dedicated book editors."

The July 27 Book Review was the last one. From now on, it will be another sub-section in the Calendar section. Art Seidenbaum, Robert Kirsch, and the many others who made the section what it was must be turning in their respective graves.

Steve Wasserman, a former editor of the *Times'* book review section, recently interviewed on WNYC, New York's flagship public radio station, said: "One thing the Internet has demonstrated is that there is a considerable hunger and avidity for cultural news of all kinds, not least of which is news of books. And books, I must say, have yet to be bested as the single most accessible instrument for the conveyance of deep knowledge and lasting entertainment. And the news of those books should be promoted, in my judgment, by the newspapers whose purpose it is to provide the news of the day."

Crime writer and former *Times* reporter, Michael Connolly, who has authored 17 books, wrote: "In the past, newspaper executives understood the symbiotic relationship between their product and books. People who read books also read newspapers. From that basic tenet came a philosophy: If you foster books, you foster reading. If you foster reading, you foster newspapers…What I fear is that…efforts to cut costs now will damage both books and newspapers in the future. Short-term gains will become long-term losses."

On July 27, the last day of the *Times* book review section, there were eight pages of the comics section.

For years I've collected historic newspapers, a collection now numbering in excess of 150. The oldest is the *Gloucester Journal* of August 1, 1738.

There's a quasi-macabre subset in the collection: the last edition of newspapers. I have the final efforts of the *Minneapolis Star*, the *Los Angeles Herald-Examiner*, the *Hollywood Citizen-News*, the *Washington Star*, the *Philadelphia Bulletin*, and several more. Now I'll have to add the *Times* book review section to the collection.

I may continue to read you, *Los Angeles Times*, but I don't love you any more.

***

> *Were it left to me to decide whether we should have a government without newspapers, or newspapers without a government, I should not hesitate a moment to prefer the latter.*
> —President Thomas Jefferson

(Photo Credit: Los Angeles Valley College Historical Museum)

Signing the Boulder Dam Power Contract in April 1930 are (seated, l.-r.): W.P. Whitsett, Chairman of the Board, Metropolitan Water District, and John R. Haynes, Board of Water and Power Commissioners. Standing behind them are officials from the MWD; Edison Co.; the U.S. Bureau of Reclamation; Los Angeles Power Bureau; and the U.S. Department of the Interior.

Water – Not Oil – Will be Source of Conflict

I caught my first fish (a scrawny catfish) in Philadelphia's Schuylkill River.

I first swam in the ocean off the Atlantic City shore.

I threw my first snowball at my best friend Johnnie Greco half a century ago.

I fearfully endured a hard landing on the deck of an aircraft carrier as part of the Navy's Leaders to Sea program.

Funny how many of the memorable moments of our lives have a connection to water.

Since we evolved from aquatic creatures (sorry, creationists), it should be no surprise that water plays a central part in our lives.

But it's more important than that. Very, very literally, we can't live without it.

Even the ancients knew water would be an important issue.

Moses brought water to the thirsty Israelites (or were they Jews by then? I can never tell when the former morphed into the latter) by smoting (Moses only "smotes," never "strikes") a rock. Sadly, Charlton Heston is not here today to replicate that feat; even David Fleming couldn't alleviate our drought by smiting one of the Vasquez Rocks.

Each American consumes about 150 gallons of water daily for drinking, cooking, bathing, flushing the toilet, laundry, watering lawns and plants, and on and on. With 305,205,000 Americans, that's a lot of water over the dam.

Like water off a duck's back, to use an appropriate cliché, we keep ignoring the prophets of liquid doom who tell us that water is tomorrow's oil, that more wars in the near future will be fought over water than land, and that we'd better start addressing the issue today if we don't want to be thirsty tomorrow.

Water is replacing oil as the likeliest cause of conflict in the Middle East.

In 1979, when President Anwar Sadat signed the peace treaty with Israel, he said Egypt will never go to war again, except to protect its water resources. Jordan's King Hussein promised he will never go to war with Israel again except over water, and the former United Nations Secretary General bluntly warned that the next war in the area will be over water.

The UN estimates that 70 percent of the water used worldwide is for agriculture. Much more will be needed to feed the world's growing population, which is predicted to rise from today's 6 billion to nearly 9 billion by 2050. If we go on as we are, millions more will go to bed hungry and thirsty each night than do now.

It's not as if our own water agencies are ignoring the problem. MWD publishes such page-turners as: *Ten Great Native and California Friendly Plants*, to *Choosing a Smart Sprinkler Controller for Your Home*, to the ever-popular *Choosing a Dual-Flush or High Efficiency Toilet for Your Home.*

Since we take our water for granted, we're likely to keep doing so...unless we are hit over the head, or in our wallets. It took steep gasoline price increases to get us to move toward smaller, more efficient automobiles.

A June 7 article in the *New York Times* pointed out that Riverside, Kern, San Louis Obispo, and Santa Barbara Counties, "have begun denying, delaying or challenging authorization for dozens of housing tracts and other developments under a state law that requires a 20-year water supply as a condition for building."

How about if we raise the price of commercial, industrial, agricultural and residential water 25 percent a year? Then we take all that extra money and put it into implementing alternate strategies, such as desalination, that already exist.

Humans can develop buildings, improve technology, and build cars and planes...but we haven't discovered how to create water...and we're not likely to. But with the majority of our planet covered with water, we CAN make the oceans serve as the source of the water we need.

There are over 21,000 desalination plants worldwide, producing over 3.5 billion gallons of potable water a day. Desalination equipment is now in use in more than 120 countries, including Australia, China, Greece,

India, Italy, Japan, Portugal, Spain, and many more. Saudi Arabia leads the world in desalination and relies on it to meet 70 percent of the country's drinking water needs.

Here in Southern California, two projects are slowly winding their way through the maze of regulations and restrictions we place on anything new, one in Carlsbad and one in Huntington Beach.

According to its developers: "The $300 million Carlsbad Desalination Project will have significant economic benefits for the region, including an estimated $170 million in spending during construction, 2,100 jobs created during construction and $37 million in annual spending throughout the region once the desalination plant is operational."

Most important of all, it will be a small step to addressing the ever-present Southern California drought.

If the ostrich gets thirsty enough, he'll bury his head looking for water.

***

> *Anyone who can solve the problems of water will be worthy of two Nobel prizes – one for peace and one for science.*
> —President John F. Kennedy

Terrible Trio Takes its Toll but This Too Shall Pass

The sky really **is** falling, Chicken Little!

Our north-of-Mulholland and slightly-south-of-Paradise community is being tested mightily with a trio of trials. Two of the three are strictly local, while the third is running rampant around the globe.

The crash of Metro 111 in Chatsworth, the disastrous fires in the Porter Ranch and Lake View Terrace areas, and the international economic meltdown...combined, they are enough to give the staunchest Valley heart a measure of misery.

The ever-larger TV screens that sit in our living rooms, with the every-blemish-revealing clarity of high definition, only enhance the horror of twisted metal and the mountains of flame and innocent-looking-but-deadly showers of embers occurring but a few miles from our homes.

It was less than two months ago, on September 12, that a Metrolink commuter train hurtled down the tracks and plowed into a Union Pacific freight locomotive, killing 25 people and injuring 135. It was the nation's worst train accident since 1993.

From all preliminary reports, the head-on accordioning of the two trains was the result of the passenger train's engineer texting instead of engineering. Will it serve as a wake-up call for all those people who still misuse their cell phones while operating vehicles? Don't bet on it.

And almost exactly one month to the day after those two trains collided in a mechanical kiss of death, the northern end of the Valley exploded in flame.

Our annual fall recipe of Santa Ana winds, end-of-summer heat, and low humidity once again whipped up an unwanted desert of destruction. We heard not the Snap! Crackle! and Pop! of Rice Krispies, but of dry chaparral and brush exploding into fiery flame.

Displaced residents, terrified horses, property in peril – we've seen them all before...and no doubt will again.

And yet, amidst the heat and hell of both disasters, our emergency responders – police, firefighters, and paramedics – did their jobs, not just well, but consummately well.

The third of the Terrible Trio we have had to endure is the national and international financial meltdown. The eyes glaze over, the brain atrophies, and the hands go clammy when trying to understand the complexities that caused the precipitous decline of the stock market.

Look at the empty storefronts along the Valley's commercial streets, notice how non-profits are scrambling more than ever to overcome shortfalls in contributions, listen to the sounds of your investments hitting the floor with a sickening thud.

And the struggles Mr. Everybusinessman faces are exacerbated by the unconscionable severance packages and buyout bonuses departing failed corporate executives take away, not the least being this column's favorite whipping boy, the former honcho at Countrywide Financial, as well as the likes of Merrill Lynch's Chairman and CEO Stanley O'Neal and Citigroup's head Charles Prince.

Our collective angst is only exacerbated by the seemingly-never-ending Presidential race, with its tinges of racism and sexism, and overt negativism.

Depressed yet?

Well, don't bet against the resilience of the Valley's businesses and residents. After the Northridge Earthquake and many other fires and traumas, we picked ourselves up, dusted ourselves off, and started all over again.

The film from which that song came was a Fred Astaire-Ginger Rogers bit of fluff from 1936, *Swing Time*. That was the height of the Depression, a time in which Americans faced rougher times than we now, or will, face. These Dorothy Fields lyrics are worth thinking about, 72 years on:

Now nothing's impossible I've found, for when my chin is on the ground,
I pick myself up, dust myself off, and start all over again.
Don't lose your confidence if you slip, be grateful for a pleasant trip,
And pick yourself up, dust yourself off, start all over again.

Work like a soul inspired until the battle of the day is won.
You may be sick and tired, but you be a man, my son.
Will you remember the famous men who have to fall to rise again,
So take a deep breath, pick yourself up, start all over again.

The Metro trains are running again, the vegetation turned to ash in the fires will regenerate itself, and destroyed property will be rebuilt.

Even now, we can hope that the Economic Alliance, UCC, the Valley's chambers of commerce, VEDC, and other organizations, are working, individually and in tandem, to help rebuild the economy in our little corner of the world.

We still have the word's greatest weather, a diverse business base, and a hard-working and well-trained workforce. All we have to do it pick ourselves up, dust ourselves off, and start all over again.

***

All we have to fear is fear itself.
—President Franklin D. Roosevelt

Ninety Years Ago this Month, but Only a Fleeting Memory

Here it is November, and yet once again we have let Veterans Day slip by with barely a salute.

On November 11, I plan to drive Ventura Boulevard from Sepulveda Boulevard to Topanga Canyon Boulevard and count the number of American flags.

Our collective memory in this country lasts but a nanosecond, unless it is something important, such as who won last season's *American Idol*, how much the Dow Jones fell yesterday, or how quickly Britney Spears' hair is growing back.

Perhaps we should be ashamed of ourselves. Our ability to honor through remembrance those who gave their lives for our country is minimal and usually limited to seeing a TV clip or newspaper photograph of flag-festooned graves at our local VA cemetery.

The roll call of dead American soldiers is testament to man's inability to become more civilized: World War I: 116,516; World War II: 405,039; Korean War: 54,246; Vietnam: 90,209.

There is just one Doughboy left. Frank Woodruff Buckles of Charles Town, West Virginia, was born

February 1, 1901, and is the last living American veteran from WWI.

Veterans Days, or as we used to call it, Armistice Day, began with "The War to End all Wars," exactly ninety years ago, on November 11, 1918. Major hostilities of World War I were formally ended at the 11th hour of the 11th day of the 11th month of 1918 when the Germans signed an Armistice, at Rethondes, France.

On November 11, 1920, the British interred their Unknown Soldier in Westminster Abbey while the French laid theirs to rest on the same day beneath the Arch de Triomphe. On November 11, 1921, an unknown World War I American soldier was buried in Arlington National Cemetery.

For years, business would come to a halt for two minutes at 11 a.m. on the 11th day of the 11th month. But now we are too busy to devote two minutes to honor our dead American soldiers.

But they do it right in Israel.

I was there in 2005, on that nation's Memorial Day. Yom Hazikaron commemorates Israel's 22,437 fallen soldiers and victims of terrorism.

For 24 hours, from sunset to sunset, theaters, cinemas, nightclubs, pubs, etc. are closed. All radio and television stations broadcast special programs and Israeli songs that convey the mood of the day. A siren blares across the country twice, during which the entire nation observes a two-minute standstill.

I watched what appeared like a scene out of an old *Twilight Zone* episode: When the siren blared, all traffic ground to a halt. Pedestrians stopped where they were on sidewalks, or even in the middle of crossing a street. Everyone stood absolutely still for two minutes.

Why is it that among Americans displays of patriotism come more easily from those in uniform than from civilians?

Army Reserve Chaplain Jim Higgins is Senior Pastor of McEachern Memorial United Methodist Church in Powder Springs, Georgia. He wrote this letter home in May 2007, while stationed at Camp Anaconda, a large U.S. base near Balad, Iraq:

"...We have a large auditorium we use for movies... We stood and snapped to attention when the National Anthem began before the main feature. All was going as planned until about three-quarters of the way through the National Anthem the music stopped.

"Now, what would happen if this occurred with 1,000 18-22 year-olds back in the States? I imagine there would be hoots, catcalls, laughter, a few rude comments... Here, the 1,000 Soldiers continued to stand at attention, eyes fixed forward. The music started again. The Soldiers continued to quietly stand at attention. And again, at the same point, the music stopped...

"You could have heard a pin drop. Every Soldier continued to stand at attention. Suddenly there was a lone voice, then a dozen, and quickly the room was filled with the voices of a thousand soldiers, finishing where the recording left off: *'And the rockets red glare, The bombs bursting in air, Gave proof through the night That our flag was still there. Oh, say does that star-spangled banner yet wave, O'er the land of the free, And the home of the brave.'*

"It was the most inspiring moment I have had here in Iraq. I wanted you to know what kind of Soldiers are serving you here. Remember them as they fight for you! For many have already paid the ultimate price."

I'll drive down Ventura Boulevard again next year on November 11. Maybe a few more of you will fly the American Flag.

***

> *This nation will remain the land of the free only so long as it is the home of the brave.*
> —Elmer Davis
> Journalist/Author

A November Ritual We Can Do Without

The devastation of fire is catastrophic, capricious, and all-consuming.

It is also just about the scariest thing we face here in the Valley and the rest of the city.

The recent spate of fires ranging from Montecito to Orange and Riverside Counties has brought home to us once again how Mother Nature can exert her ascendancy over us at will. As of this writing, these mid-November fires have resulted in more than 1,000 homes destroyed and more than 25,000 acres burned.

My first truly major LA fire was unforgettable.

As a young UCLA student in November of 1961, I remember standing atop Royce Hall looking out at the flames as they raced across a ridgeline in sight of campus. Eighty-five percent of all the Los Angeles Fire Department's resources were thrown against the Bel-Air fire.

Robert Fovell, an associate professor of atmospheric and oceanic sciences at UCLA said that, "If you wanted to design a climate that was conducive to fire hazard, you invent Southern California. Here's the recipe: wet in the winter, long hot summer, and Santa Ana winds in the fall."

Just like the conflagrations of this year, the deadly combination of Santa Ana winds, intense heat, and dry post-summer brush, created the perfect recipe for tragedy. By the time the Bel-Air fire was defeated, 484 – mostly very expensive – residences were destroyed.

The Porter Ranch and Lake View Terrace infernos (or, to use their technical terms, the Sesnon and Marek fires) are just two more in a long line of November blazes that have victimized Our Valley. Between them, more than 15,000 acres went up in flames.

The eleventh month is clearly accursed when it comes to fires in the Valley, as evidenced by these conflagrations, all of which occurred in November: Old Topanga Fire (1993), Topanga Canyon Fire (1977), La Tuna Canyon Fire (1955).

Like all catastrophic events, the best and worst of us is brought out by fire.

We all warm to the images of food and drink brought out to the firefighters by grateful residents where they are engaged in combat. Elected officials unceasingly talk about the bravery and commitment of the area's firefighters...but even unceasing praise is not enough. Imagine going into the flames in those bulky, hot, firefighting suits, endangering your life at every turn, and knowing that nearly every fire you fight can outrun you.

And the spirit of community is heightened by these disasters: One of our local channels showed a front yard near the Montecito fire filled with clothing and canned goods, with a big sign: "Need it? Take it." If that doesn't make you feel better about your fellow man, nothing will.

On the other hand, the arrest of two women found looting a near-burnt-out mobile home in the Oakridge Mobile Home Park that was one of more than 500 destroyed in this month's Sylmar fire epitomizes the levels to which some people can sink.

"Take 'em out and shoot 'em," was once suggested by a police official during the Watts Riots, speaking of looters. Maybe a bit harsh; but not by much.

The Bel-Air fire was more than 45 years ago. Here is just part of the lengthy analysis of that fire, from the Los Angeles Fire Department Historical Archive:

"Persistent efforts have been made by the fire department to secure ordinance changes that would effectively reduce the mushrooming conflagration hazard. To date, no legislation has been enacted to specifically counter this peculiar and dire peril in the mountainous portions of the city. The ravaged dwellings in Bel-Air and Brentwood remain a depressing monument to this fact.

"The people living in these regions will receive a maximum degree of security from fire only when reasonable and enforceable laws are produced to effectively regulate and control unsafe structural practices, brush clearance around buildings, water distribution, and accessibility within the mountain areas. Once a conflagration has begun, the best-trained fire fighters, most modern apparatus, and best tactical procedures can only struggle to restrict losses... No responsible fire authority can give assurance that a conflagration will not occur while, at the same time, terrible conflagration conditions are permitted to exist.

"If the Bel-Air and Brentwood disasters are not to be repeated in the future, it is mandatory that conflagrations be attacked in the most intelligent manner – before they have a chance to begin."

While progress has been made on some of these fronts, are our Mayor and 15 City Council members ready to look us in our collective eyes and tell us that everything that could be done has been done to minimize the likelihood of a repeat of the Valley's November fires?

***

Firemen never die, they just burn forever in the hearts of the people whose lives they saved.
—Susan Diane Murphree
Federation of Fire Chaplains

May I Have a Word With You?

Words can soar and swoop; inspire and inflame; turn a champ into a chump.

Words are the building blocks of thoughts, the bricks and mortar of ideas that shape our lives, our society, and our universe.

Words can unite us and divide us.

Taking the Orange Line to a meeting recently I heard three women conversing excitedly in Spanish; a pair of students who alighted from the vehicle at Valley College speaking in German; and what appeared to be an elderly man and his daughter bickering in what I believed to be Armenian.

And I didn't understand a word of any of it.

I felt as if I were in the middle of a Tower of Babel on wheels.

Words – and the use of them to inspire others – are the exclusive province of neither the good nor of the evil. Could anyone inspire good better than Winston Churchill? Could anyone inspire evil better than Adolph Hitler?

Both would have believed writer Joseph Conrad when he said, "Give me the right word...and I will move the world."

Teddy Roosevelt could pound his bully pulpit like no one else in his early-twentieth-century world, while no one could be more soothing than his fifth cousin, Franklin Roosevelt, in his wartime Fireside Chats.

Nathanial Hawthorne might have been referring to the Churchills and Hitlers and Roosevelts of the world when he wrote that "Words ... how potent for good and evil they become in the hands of one who knows how to combine them."

Melvyn Bragg, whose English radio series, *The Routes of English*, traced the course of spoken English, said: "'The nation had the lion's heart. I had the luck to give the roar,' Churchill is reported once to have said about his pivotal role in the Second World War. But the roar that he gave the country was far more than sound – it was...a subtle mixture of words and delivery, of voice, vocal pyrotechnics, and a deep understanding of the power of language that was unique."

But sadly, much of American business, and the lawyers whose opinions are usually taken as Words from On High, too often use language to obfuscate, complicate, and even excuse.

Here, for example, is just one sentence in a document that many of us recently received in the mail from AT&T, entitled Residential Service Agreement:

"You agree that AT&T, our employees, officers, directors, affiliates, subsidiaries, assignees and agents, shall not be responsible for any claims, demands, actions, causes of action, suits proceedings, losses, damages, costs and expenses, including reasonable attorney fees, arising from or relating to any use of any services, or any action, error, or omission in connection therewith, by you or any person you authorize or permit to use any services including but not limited to matters relating to: incorrect, incomplete or misleading information, defamation, libel or slander; invasion of privacy; name, trademark, service mark, or other intellectual property; any defective product or service sold or otherwise distributed through or in connection with any services or any injury or damage to person or property caused thereby; or violation of any applicable law or regulation (collectively 'Losses')."

One sentence; 133 words long.

And, if I may say, hopefully without jeopardizing delivery of my home telephone service, exceedingly boring, not to mention overwhelmingly obtuse. The entire document is more than 7,800 words of equally unintelligible legalese.

Those of you still awake and lucid after reading that sentence are invited to finish this column; I promise you no sentence more than 55 words long.

I asked an executive of AT&T what that sentence meant, and after giving me a slightly sheepish grin, he said, "It sounds as if you as a customer cannot sue AT&T unless there is any willful or gross negligence on the part of AT&T."

He is, of course, right...and why couldn't have AT&T's communicators (and I use the word exceedingly loosely) just have written that?

Imagine if AT&T's corporate lawyer/copyrighters had been afforded the opportunity to put into legalese, "Give me liberty or give me death!" Or "Make my day." Or "Ich bin ein Berliner." Or "Mr. Gorbachev, tear down this wall."

As all of these examples prove, simple words do not equate to simple thoughts.

Our sixth President, John Quincy Adams, wrote that "Slovenly language corrodes the mind." He could have also written that unclear and deliberately difficult-to-comprehend language equally corrodes the mind.

To those who believe that a simple sentence is inferior to compound or complex sentences, may I recommend the writings of Al Martinez in the *Los Angeles Times*, Ernest Hemingway, or Andy Rooney...now *there's* a diverse trio. But they all have one thing in common, they write simply and succinctly, and communicate clearly.

Got it?

And one final sentence: Happy Holidays.

***

> *The difference between the right word and the almost right word is like the difference between lightning and the lightning bug.*
> —Mark Twain

Youngsters from the Boys & Girls Club of the West Valley surround me after selecting their books at the annual Cooper Reading Challenge. In 2009, 152 children, many from disadvantaged circumstances, were each given $25 from Club supporters to buy books at Borders.

A Trip to the Bookstore: Reading, Redux

Some things are so good they're worth doing again.

Last year, to commemorate the 25th anniversary of my firm, we donated $25 to each of 25 children from the Boys & Girls Club of the West Valley.

Many of these youngsters come from single-parent homes, are economically disadvantaged, or live in an environment where English is minimally spoken, if at all. The Club's goal is to give them more positive life options.

After I wrote about the Cooper Reading Challenge in this column last year, many of you contacted me and said that if I ever did it again, you'd love to participate.

Well, since I don't hold out high hopes to being at the helm of Cooper Communications 25 years from now to celebrate a 50th anniversary, I decided to do it again this year. And we did, just before Christmas/Hanukkah/Kwanzaa (to be completely inclusive).

Thanks to many of our friends, last year's 25 children getting books became this year's 96 youngsters. Just a few who contributed so that one or more children could buy books for themselves were: Club supporter and noted actor Hector Elizondo; AT&T's Kevin Tamaki;

A Trip to the Bookstore: Reading, Redux

First Commerce Bank's Wendy Moskal; CSUN's Andrea Reinken; and several members of the Club's Board.

The Club invited all of its 2,500 youngsters to participate by reading an age-appropriate book and then write a review of what they had read. The staff selected the best.

Each child received $25 to buy one or more books. (No CDs, not DVDs, not calendars, just books.) There was no overhead or anything else taken out; every dollar contributed went directly to a child to buy books. Borders gave the Club's youngsters a 20 percent discount and provided them with snacks to help make this a memorable experience.

Many of those who donated enhanced their personal involvement by going with us to help the children pick out their books, and that provided an extra degree of interaction between the donors and recipients. There were so many youngsters who participated that it took three separate trips to the book store to accommodate them all.

There was rampant enthusiasm among all the children. One little girl was so happy she ran up one aisle and down another, flapping her arms and yelling, "I'm so excited!"

As we were helping the children select their books, I thought of Maya Angelou's quote: "If I were a young person today, trying to gain a sense of myself in the world, I would do that again by reading, just as I did when I was young."

A few vignettes from our Borders trips:

A young girl, about eight, said that she wanted to buy a book for her big brother for Christmas. When queried what he was interested in, she said, "He likes animals and cars; can we find a book about both animals and cars?" She settled for a book on vintage Chevrolets. I wanted to point out a picture of a Chevy Impala — thereby meeting her cars **and** animals criterion – but I resisted the temptation.

One of the Club's teen-age members selected a more-than-500-page edition of Margaret Mitchell's *Gone with the Wind*. When asked if that was too long a book for her, she gave the questioner a withering look of disdain. She was deeply engrossed in the first chapter while standing in the check-out line.

One high-school-age youngster, as soon as he walked into the store said, "I've never been to a bookstore before...what do I do now?" He'll never have to ask that question again.

When asked what kind of books he was looking for, Kevin whipped out a written list he had prepared. He had even called Borders in advance to make sure his selections were available.

Ten-year-old Haley, who attends Ivy Academia, bragged about having read all 752 pages of *The Count of Monte Cristo*. He walked out with a large book on World War II, telling all who would listen about his uncle's service in the Vietnam War.

Natalie, a 14-year-old student at Northridge Academy, wins the Cooper Award for Selflessness. She selected a Spanish-English Bible for her mother. When it was pointed out to her that the bilingual Bible was $25 and that she wouldn't have any money left over to buy a book for herself, she said that was just fine. The Bible was what her mother wanted for Christmas, and that was what she was getting. I hope Natalie's mom appreciates her.

Like all of you, I was gifted – and regifted – with several holiday baskets filled with goodies I'll probably never consume. None of them came close to providing the pleasure and warm feelings we all received from the simple act of helping children pick out books.

***

There is no substitute for books in the life of a child.
—Mary Ellen Chase
Author of more than 30 books

Billy: He's an Elephant WE Won't Forget

This month I was going to write about an important issue.

The choices included the continuing international economic meltdown and how it is affecting San Fernando Valley businesses; the inability of our elected leaders in Sacramento to agree on a budget for California; or the mushrooming local deficit and its consequences for Los Angeles.

But those topics all took a back seat to the most burning topic of the day: 23-year-old Billy the Elephant.

Now, I like elephants just as much as the next person.

They're peaceful, lumbering giants who never forget a thing. It has been their sad lot to be the victims of poachers who would kill, and often do, for elephant tusks. They have been subjected to abuses on the part of circuses. But perhaps one of the greatest indignities foisted upon one of these mammoth (forgive the pun) mammals is the recent brouhaha over the lone elephant now inhabiting the Los Angeles Zoo.

The $42 million Pachyderm Forest at the Los Angeles Zoo was first approved by the City Council in 2006. Early this year, the Council voted to suspend work on the exhibit, a third of which is complete. And then, on January 28, the Council voted 11 to four to complete the six-acre Pachyderm Forest

The final debate lasted more than four hours. That's right, four hours! Can anyone remember a four-hour discussion in City Council about gangs, traffic congestion, the City's disastrous budgetary situation, or any of the myriad concerns Angelinos have expressed?

Hats off to Councilmember Bill Rosendahl who said during the Council debate, "I hope we spend four hours on the homeless, gridlock and other issues that affect our city."

And then there's the financial side of the equation...

Los Angeles has already spent $12 million of the $42 million project estimate. Shutting down the project would have forced the City to repay $5 million in bond money, while completing the Pachyderm Forest will cost the City $1.2 million a year in debt payments for 20 years, or a total of $24 million.

The Greater Los Angeles Zoo Association, a nonprofit support group, has, to date, donated $4.8 million to the project and pledged an additional $6 million, which, theoretically, will allow the City to borrow that much less money, and therefore reduce the debt payments.

So, the City will have to spend – give or take – a mere $18 million to give Billy a home.

For $18 million, how many needy people could be fed and clothed by MEND; how many people dealing with autism and other developmental disabilities could be provided services by New Horizons; how many young people could have a safe, productive after-school experience at the Boys & Girls Club of the West Valley?

For $18 million how many more police officers could LAPD Deputy Chief Michel Moore deploy to enhance public safety in the Valley?

For $18 million how many traffic signals could be synchronized along our major boulevards?

But only four Council members voted against the expenditure: Tony Cardenas, Bernard Parks, Jan Perry, and Dennis Zine.

In an "only in LA" moment, the debate has featured such elephant experts as Cher, Halle Berry, Bob Barker, Lily Tomlin, Robert Culp, Goldie Hawn, and Kevin Nealon, most of whom, of course, have years of experience in dealing with creatures with thick hides.

The Los Angeles Zoo's official website, which has espoused the case for the Pachyderm Forest, includes the heartwarming story of Slash (formerly of Guns N' Roses) visiting the zoo and promoting completion of the project. Based on his vast knowledge of animal life, he is quoted on the website as compellingly saying, "I just want everybody to try to support this cause because it's very important."

That sure tugged at my heartstrings.

But if there's one person who really knows what she's talking about when it comes to elephants, it's Dame Daphne Sheldrick, chairperson of the David Sheldrick Wildlife Trust in Kenya, the recipient of numerous awards for her wildlife conservation work. CBS' *60 Minutes* has aired two highly positive stories about her and her successes in saving elephants.

Her wildlife refuge has successfully rehabilitated more than 70 orphan elephants. She wrote of the Pachyderm Forest controversy:

"It has been scientifically established that elephants are 'human' in terms of emotion, a finding I wholeheartedly endorse. Gregarious creatures, they have a strong sense of family and of death; they form friendships that span a lifetime. Like humans, they need the companionship and comfort of friends. Billy has been alone since May 2007, when his companion, Ruby, the zoo's last African elephant, was relocated to the Performing Animal Welfare Society's 75-acre sanctuary in San Andreas, Calif. Billy should be released to join her there.

"No artificial situation, however attractive it may appear to us human onlookers, can possibly afford a captive elephant the space it needs...Elephants are like us. They suffer from trauma and stress and, because of this, die younger in captivity. Perhaps the Los Angeles Zoo will extend compassion by releasing its elephant and affording him a little happiness as a New Year's gift. I do hope so."

Call me crazy, but when it comes to what's best for elephants, I'm more likely to believe Dame Sheldrick than Slash.

I guess the majority of our City Council doesn't see it that way.

* * *

> *Nature's great masterpiece, an Elephant.*
> *The only harmless great thing; the giant*
> *of beasts.*
> —John Donne
Author

White Hats and Black Hats

Fading into the soft, warm comfortable glow of nostalgia are the cowboys of a simpler time.

Featured in movies from the '30s to the '50s, then taking up aural residence in our living room radio consoles, and finally riding across the screens of television sets, these denizens of an Old West who never really existed were easily identified by the color of their hats that told us whether they were heroes or villains.

The good guys wore white hats; the bad guys wore black hats.

On the "good guy" side of the ledger was Tom Mix. He always wore a white ten-gallon hat, and was often shown astride his steed known as (don't laugh) Tony the Wonder Horse. Mix appeared in more than 300 Western films and subsequently spent 20 years riding the radio range. The Lone Ranger, Roy Rogers, Gene Autry, John Wayne – all the authentic ersatz movie cowboys – wore white up top.

In the famous photograph of the real Butch Cassidy, the Sundance Kid, and their partners in crime known as the Hole in the Wall Gang, every one of them was photographed wearing a black hat.

White hats good; black hats bad – that's how we'd like life to be in our 21st century world, including in Our Valley.

Some of our "white hats" are Rickey Gelb, Mel Kohn, Gary Thomas, and everyone who works at one of our many non-profit organizations for sub-prime salaries in return for above-prime fulfillment.

This column bestowed a Lifetime Black Hat Award on Angelo Mozilo long before his company, Countrywide Financial, hit the skids...and skidded over many of us.

The media helps us identify who wears white hats and black hats.

Chesley B. Sullenberger III – what an unlikely name for a hero! Captain "Sully" Sullenberger, who landed US Airways Flight 1549 safely smack dab in the middle of New York's Hudson River wears, and deservedly so, a major white hat.

Nadya Suleman, who now can boast of more than a football team's worth of children, and the doctor who gave her *in vitro* fertilization despite the fact that she already had six children, definitely wear black hats.

Bernie Madoff, whose last name should have warned us that he'd "made off" with the savings of tens of thousands of trusting folks, including numerous Jewish charities, is in a special category – he gets to wear not a black hat, but a black *yarmulke*.

And there are collective black hats worn by almost everyone who worked for the tainted, tattered talents of Wall Street, taking the last morsels of food from America's widows and orphans while dining sumptuously at Masa, Le Bernadin, Le Cirque, and Per Se.

Why the tendency to categorize everyone with a black hat or a white one? Because we crave simplicity in a complex world. By retreating into a place where the good guys and bad guys are easily identifiable, we don't have to deal with our real – and often scary – environment.

Many Valley businesspeople know that business is bad: consumers are buying less (visit any near-empty mall in Glendale, Sherman Oaks, or Woodland Hills for verification); real estate is unreal; construction has dropped faster than a ball peen hammer; and reservations at Café Bizou, Roy's, Asanebo, and Pinot Bistro are easy to come by.

Over breakfast at Cici's Café in Tarzana, California United Bank President David Rainer tried to explain to me the complexities of the current banking situation and its impact on financial markets around the world. And while I sport at least an average IQ, my eyes soon glazed over trying to understand the complexities of it all.

Derivatives, structured investment vehicles, collateralized bond obligations, master liquidity enhancement conduits – these are the terms being thrown around by Wall Street's wicked wizards. But, as we also discovered, they're more like the Wizard of Oz, who was not really a great and powerful wizard with a green face spewing smoke but merely a trembling Frank Morgan at a microphone behind a curtain.

We look for financial salvation from our elected gurus in Washington, D.C., while all the time fearing that they don't really understand what they're voting for... or against. They talk about investing millions, billions, and even trillions of dollars, as if they could just take the New York Subway down to the Federal Reserve Bank on Wall Street and melt down a few more gold bars.

How did we get here? How do we get out of it? What will it cost? Who has the answers? How will all this money being thrown at the recession benefit me?

It's all too confusing to most of us.

A lot of people are hoping that a black man named Barack Obama will wind up wearing a white hat.

***

A billion here, a billion there, pretty soon it adds up to real money.
—Everett Dirksen
Former Illinois Republican Senator

America's Newspapers are Dying. So What?

The financial wizards who have been empowered to address our economic woes do more than just testify before Congress and appear on every talk show they can find.

They tell us who's "too big to fail."

General Motors, whose Hummer is the poster child for conspicuous consumption and meaningless macho, is "too big to fail."

AIG, which bears more than a bit of the blame for the mess we're in, is "too big to fail."

I guess size does matter to today's bureaucrats.

But does anyone say of America's great but endangered newspapers, "They're too *important* to fail?"

The *Seattle Post-Intelligencer*, published from 1863 (that's before the Civil War was over) until last month. Its online progeny's news staff has 20 professionals, compared with the now-defunct print version, which had 165.

The *Rocky Mountain News* ceased publishing on February 27, after nearly 150 years.

The once-venerable (it hasn't really been "venerable" since Tribune Company bought it from the Chandlers) *Los Angeles Times*, and its sister paper, the *Chicago Tribune*, are part of a corporation in Chapter 11.

Community papers, while generally faring better than their big-city metropolitan counterparts, are not always successful. Here in Our Valley, the Sun trio (Studio City, Sherman Oaks, and Encino) ceased publication late last year.

In the past, when we'd speak about a newspaper folding, it meant halving its size; today it has a totally different meaning. The complete list of newspapers that have failed or are in bankruptcy is depressingly long.

But why should we care?

It's not about the nostalgia for an old brand; the tradition of reading the paper over the morning jolt of java; the delivery system for great columnists; it's about the absolute necessity for the role of watchdog that newspapers play in our society.

There are plenty of news source out there. Thirty minutes of network news each evening, all-news radio stations, all-news cable services, online news sources and blogs... a virtual glut of news.

But are we getting more than headlines, opinion, and subjective reportage designed to promote a preconceived point of view?

Rarely.

But what about the daily newspaper's other features?

Sports? There's more coverage of actual event on TV than the newspapers have ever brought us.

Entertainment? Sensationalistic as it is, there's plenty of that around...although what we get is more of where Lindsay Lohan is clubbing this week than how those in the industry in Los Angeles are faring in these days of runaway production.

Columnists? We can still read Al Martinez and others online, through their blogs, or community papers like the *West Valley News*.

Reviews of movies, restaurants, plays, and books? Nope; also plenty online.

Editorials, op-ed pieces, and letters to the editor? No, we're saturated with opinion from Bill O'Reilly to Jon Stewart to Rush Limbaugh.

What we're all going to be poorer without can be summed up in two words: investigative journalism.

Both historically and currently, no other medium has come close to meeting the standard of investigative journalism brought to us by that perilously endangered newspaper thrown on our driveway each morning.

When it comes to elected officials acquiring or spending money inappropriately (and in many cases, illegally); big business failing to recall a product they know is dangerous because it's profitable; or labor bosses living luxuriously on the funds they've skimmed from the union; no one does the job like a newspaper.

Just in the past few weeks, the *Los Angeles Times,* which has received more than a bit of skewering from this column, has broken stories on fraud in in-home care programs; more-than-questionable expenditures by State Senator Gil Cedillo; seemingly cavalier ignoring of California's Brown Act by elected bodies; the resignation of Carrie Lopez, the director of the state's Department of Consumer Affairs for using government money inappropriately; the exposure of Tyrone Freeman of the SEIU union for misappropriating funds for his own use; and perhaps almost humorously, the necessity of our Board of Supervisors to have water bottles labeled with their own logo.

Why are newspapers important?

Just read the official Pulitzer Prize citations awarded to newspapers for investigative journalism over the past four years, and ask yourself what other news source would provide the resources and commitment to bring these stories to light:

- 2008: "Walt Bogdanich and Jake Hooker of the *New York Times* for their stories on toxic ingredients in medicine and other everyday products imported from China, leading to crackdowns by American and Chinese officials."

- 2008: "Staff of *Chicago Tribune* for its exposure of faulty governmental regulation of toys, car seats and cribs, resulting in the extensive recall of hazardous products and congressional action to tighten supervision."

- 2007: "Brett Blackledge of *The Birmingham News* for his exposure of cronyism and corruption in the state's two-year college system, resulting in the dismissal of the chancellor and other corrective action."

- 2006: "Susan Schmidt, James V. Grimaldi and R. Jeffrey Smith of the *Washington Post* for their indefatigable probe of Washington lobbyist Jack Abramoff that exposed congressional corruption and produced reform efforts."

- 2005: "Nigel Jaquiss of *Willamette Week*, Portland, Oregon for his investigation exposing a former governor's long concealed sexual misconduct with a 14-year-old girl."

We should care about the near-demise of the American newspaper not because there are no other news sources, but because major daily newspapers have been the public's eyes and ears, exposing corruption, mismanagement, government excess, and scams.

***

Four hostile newspapers are more to be feared than a thousand bayonets.
—Napoleon Bonaparte

There's not much I've done that was more fun than producing the Playboy Jazz Festival at the Hollywood Bowl for four years. Here I am on stage with the legendary Count Basie.

Hail the American Song Book

OK, let's admit it; it's pretty bad out there.

The Democrats and Republicans in Sacramento and Washington are more interested in making the other party look bad than in solving our problems.

Unemployment is rising and stocks are falling.

Real estate is unreal.

There are floods in North Dakota and drought in Southern California.

Car sales are in the tank.

Any account called a 401(k) should be renamed a 401(bk).

We've all been singing the blues lately.

Not much left to do but turn to the panacea that's been helping Americans get through tough times for two and one-half centuries: music.

From Afro-Cuban to zydeco, with stops along the way at ragtime, rock, and rap, we have celebrated our national highs and acknowledged our national lows with music.

From Louis Armstrong to Frank Zappa, what other country has ever produced the range of musical styles and performers to rival Scott Joplin, Benny Goodman, George Gershwin, Count Basie, Aaron Copland, Elvis Presley, Bob Dylan, Fats Domino, Duke Ellington, Lionel Hampton, Lester Flatt and Earl Scruggs, Ray Charles, Burl Ives, Woody Guthrie, The Supremes, Mahalia Jackson, Ella Fitzgerald, Barbra Streisand, Stevie Wonder, Leonard Bernstein, Beverly Sills, Aretha Franklin, Frank Sinatra, Michael Jackson, Prince, Dolly Parton, Dr. Dre, and thousands more?

And let us not forget Our Valley's own Richie Valens, a Pacoima product and forefather of the Chicano rock movement, who is being honored at VICA's Business Hall of Fame dinner next month.

American music travels well: From the raw blues of Mississippi's Muddy Waters to the California surfing safaris of the Beach Boys and from Don Ho's Hawaiian melodies to Liza Minnelli's musical paean to the Big Apple, "New York, New York."

Songs of protest against war, segregation, injustice, and cruelty have galvanized Americans to address our shortcomings as well as to trumpet our triumphs.

On January 18, 2009, 90-years-old-this-month Pete Seeger and Bruce Springsteen sang the Woody Guthrie classic, "This Land is Your Land," as the finale at Barack Obama's Inaugural concert in Washington, D.C. How fitting...and how American!

Famous contralto Marian Anderson was 42 years old when she sang before 75,000 people and a nationwide radio audience at the Lincoln Memorial on Easter Sunday, 1939.

The concert was arranged after the Daughters of the American Revolution refused to let Anderson perform at Constitution Hall because she was Black. First Lady Eleanor Roosevelt resigned from the DAR in protest and helped arrange the Lincoln Memorial concert.

The filmed record of her stirring rendition of "My Country, 'tis of Thee," also known as "America," has been replayed countless times. The concert became the defining moment of her long career.

In 1961, Anderson returned to Washington to sing the national anthem at President Kennedy's inauguration, and two years later, he bestowed the Presidential Medal of Freedom on her. This honor appropriately came one year before her farewell concert tour, which she opened, ironically, at Constitution Hall, and ended on Easter Sunday, 1965, at Carnegie Hall.

Yes, we're in the midst of a great economic shake-out here in Our Valley and across the country.

But don't sell a nation short that can produce Kate Smith belting out "God Bless America"; the Mormon Tabernacle Choir chanting "The Battle Hymn of the Republic"; and "The Boss," Bruce Springsteen, proudly pumping the air with his fist as he proudly declaims that he was "Born in the U.S.A."

And no one summed it up more simply than rock 'n' roll legend Chuck Berry, who wrote, and sang, "Back in the U.S.A.":

Well, I'm so glad I'm livin' in the U.S.A.
Yes. I'm so glad I'm livin' in the U.S.A.
Anything you want, we got right here in the U.S.A.

Teary-eyed patriotism won't get us through the challenges we have to overcome; but remembering where we've come from, who we are, and where we can yet go, will make the task easier.

Perhaps Neil Diamond reminds us best where we stand in the world:

"Everywhere around the world,
They're coming to America.
Every time that flag's unfurled
They're coming to America.

Got a dream to take them there,
They're coming to America.
Got a dream they've come to share
They're coming to America.

They're coming to America
They're coming to America
They're coming to America
They're coming to America
Today, today, today, today, today."

No one endures searing desert heat, hunger, or overcrowded boats close to capsizing, to get **out** of this country.

Those who think they hear a clock ticking down the final minutes of America's greatness may actually be listening to the steady and reliable sound of America's metronome.

***

True music must repeat the thought and inspirations of the people and the time. My people are Americans and my time is today.
—George Gershwin

(Photo Credit: Urban Archives Center. Oviatt Library. California State University, Northridge)

Hard to believe, but the Ku Klux Klan actually staged a parade on Van Nuys Boulevard as recently as September 15, 1966, less than 45 years ago.

We Americans Give Good Hate

We Americans give good hate.

Over the past 250 years we've managed to hate Native Americans, the Irish, Italians, Catholics, the Chinese (we were masters of that in Los Angeles), the Japanese, Jews, African Americans, Latinos, Communists, the French (who can forget freedom fries?), Muslims, homosexuals, and a whole lot more.

In fact, at some time, we've managed to hate just about everybody. Have a different color skin...we'll hate you. Worship differently...we'll hate you. Even vote differently...we'll hate you.

In fact, one might call us equal opportunity haters.

They say good things come in threes...evidently so do bad things.

Just in the past month we've witnessed an attack on the U.S. Memorial Holocaust Museum in Washington, D.C.; the murder of a doctor who performed abortions in Wichita, Kansas; and Reverend Jeremiah Wright, who told a columnist for the Newport News Virginia, *Daily Press*, that "them Jews ain't going to let him [President Obama] talk to me...they will not let him to talk to somebody who calls a spade what it is."

It's easy to think that hatred of people based strictly on the color of their skin, the place where they worship, or the land from which they come, is a problem faced by those far from Our Valley.

But let us not forget the beating of Rodney King (Lakeview Terrace); the 1999 attack on the North Valley Jewish Community Center (Granada Hills); the vandalizing of a string of houses of worship (Encino and Tarzana); and the defacing of Councilman Jack Weiss' office (Sherman Oaks).

We can claim a long history of hatred in Our Valley.

Before it was renamed Woodland Hills, the community at the far end of the Valley was known as Girard. Its newspaper, the *Girard News,* reported on December 27, 1924, that "San Fernando Valley churches were surprised last Sunday night when 15 Knights of the K.K.K. in full regalia visited eight Van Nuys churches and one Reseda church in a body...a leader presented the minister with an envelope...the message was a cordial season greeting and attached to each was a check for $25 made payable to the church... Enthusiastic applause greeted the gift in every instance."

CSUN's Oviatt Library Digital is a treasure trove of this history of hatred in our own community:

- There's a photograph of a Ku Klux Klan Parade on Van Nuys Boulevard on September 15, 1966.

- During the same week, a flier was widely distributed across the Valley inviting "All White Christians" to a "Gigantic Cross Burning" and rally on September 17, in Soledad Canyon. If you wanted to attend, you could contact Rev. William V. Fowler of La Crescenta.

- And then there's the late 1950s photograph of a property parcel for sale in Reseda. Three men are sitting near a sign that reads: "Lots for sale to colored only, H. G. Weaver, DI. 8-1835."

And in case you think this is all ancient history, the following is from a June 2004 post on the Storm Front's website, which defines itself as standing for "White Pride World Wide": "There are National Alliance members in the Valley. There are Aryan Nations members in the Valley. There are Creators in the Valley. There are W.A.R. members in the Valley. There are SFV Peckerwoods in the Valley. There are members of each of those groups and more."

As recently as May 3, 2006, Rachel Uranga, a *Daily News* staff writer, wrote: "'There was an unwritten policy that you didn't have a reason to be in the West Valley unless you lived there,' said the Rev. Zedar Broadus, former director of the NAACP chapter in the San Fernando Valley and lifelong resident. 'You stepped out and the police pulled you over.'

"Pacoima was the only area where blacks could buy homes in the 1950s and 1960s. Japanese returning from internment camps were forced into housing tracts in Burbank and the Northeast Valley. And in San Fernando, there was an unstated rule that most Mexicans lived on the other side of the tracks.

"Being non-white in the Valley during the decades after World War II was tough. Making matters worse, during the 1960s a neo-Nazi party found its home in Glendale and Panorama City."

Of course, we don't have a monopoly on hate.

In the mid-'30s, Martin Niemoller, one of Germany's leading anti-Nazi pastors, was arrested for treason on Hitler's direct orders. From then until the end of WW II, he was held at the Sachsenhausen and Dachau concentration camps.

In 1946, he wrote this famous poem:

First they came for the Communists, and I didn't speak up,
because I wasn't a Communist.

Then they came for the Jews, and I didn't speak up,
because I wasn't a Jew.

Then they came for the Catholics, and I didn't speak up,
because I was a Protestant.

Then they came for me,
and by that time there was no one left to speak up for me.

Reverend Niemoller outlived Hitler, dying in West Germany at the age of 92 in 1984.

As in so many other things, we Americans are state-of-the-art when it comes to hate.

Wouldn't it be more fun to be state-of-the-art in love?

***

Let us develop respect for all living things. Let us try to replace violence and intolerance with understanding and compassion. And love.
—Jane Goodall
Humanitarian

Living just up the street from the media frenzy of the Michael Jackson death and funeral brought home how intrusive wall-to-wall coverage of celebrity events can be.

No "Thriller" of a Media Event in Encino

Elvis has left the building, Michael Jackson has left the Staples Center, and we're left with sensory – and media – overload.

Those basing an opinion on the sheer volume of the media coverage afforded Michael Jackson's death would be safe to conclude that his demise spells the end of life on Earth as we know it.

Now we can look forward to near-endless – and breathless – coverage by *Entertainment Tonight, TMZ*, and all the similar mind-numbing television programs covering Jackson-related lawsuits, drug use, his burial site, and a whole host of post-mortem issues.

There is, of course, a strong Valley connection to all of this. Since the early '70s, the Jackson family home has been on Hayvenhurst Avenue in Encino, barely a white glove's throw up the street from Gelson's.

The media calls it the "Jackson Compound," as if it encompassed a palatial mansion with numerous outbuildings scattered over several acres...nothing could be further from the truth. But it sounds good.

In fact, from now on, friends are expected to speak of the "Cooper Compound" when referring to my modest domicile, located a few blocks south of the Jacksons.

From the moment of Jackson's death on June 25, fans began trekking to the "Jackson Compound" with the fervor of Muslims making their once-in-a-lifetime religious *hajj* to Mecca.

Out of pure journalistic imperative I spent some time watching our Encino version of Ringling Bros. Circus.

On the west side of the street, fans quickly erected a make-shift shrine, complete with scrawled messages, balloons, floral bouquets, and even a teddy bear or two. Most of them, quite orderly within iron barriers, tacked items up on the fences of the Jackson home's next-door neighbors (long-suffering folk they must be!) until they were a mass of color more than 30 feet wide.

An equally fascinating show unfolded on the east side of the street...a show starring the world's media.

Yours truly was in charge of media at the annual Academy Awards for ten years, but I've never seen so many huge satellite dishes in one place at one time (11, at one count). Somehow they reminded me of the aliens in H. G. Wells' *War of the Worlds*, striding relentlessly across the landscape. Hundreds – no exaggeration – of reporters, videographers, sound people, technicians, all were there to record, and report, the slightest bit of information.

Overhead, beginning at daybreak the day of the Staples Center memorial service, three or four helicopters swirled and hovered over Encino, making sure we had an unfettered aerial view of the goings-on on television, but oblivious to the infuriated residents below awakened by their noise.

While on my weekend walk (I delude myself into thinking it's part of my exercise regimen) from the Cooper Compound to the Starbucks at Ventura Boulevard and Hayvenhurst Avenue and back, still unshaven and unshowered, KABC-TV's Luanne Suter gave me my 15 seconds (not minutes, in my case) of fame. She asked me about the inconveniences of the continuing closure of Hayvenhurst, automobiles parked bumper-to-bumper on every side street, and strangers wandering through the neighborhood every hour of the night and day.

Being the consummate public relations professional, I lied through clenched teeth, muttering something about it being a minor inconvenience.

At an Encino Neighborhood Council meeting convened on July 8 in the musty but venerable Encino Woman's Club, more than one Encino resident talked about the media overkill.

Finally, at about 11 p.m. on Wednesday, July 8, the LAPD opened Hayvenhurst Ave. to through traffic.

The highly regarded Pew Research Center for the People & the Press, an independent opinion research group that studies attitudes toward the press, politics and public policy issues, looked at the Jackson media coverage (dare we say overkill?) in its most recent survey.

Their survey revealed that "nearly two-in-three Americans say news organizations gave too much coverage to the story."

A separate analysis by the Pew Research Center's Project for Excellence in Journalism showed that from the announcement of Jackson's death on Thursday to the end of the day Friday, "60 percent of the news coverage studied was devoted to his death, his life story and his legacy."

And this while protests continued in Iran, healthcare reform legislation was being considered, the California budget impasse continued unabated, Congress was debating a federal greenhouse gas bill, and a train crash in Washington, D.C., left nine people dead.

The cult of celebrity lives...even when its objects do not. When Jackson's death was reported, Google, Yahoo, and the social networks, were near-overloaded with traffic. CNN got a 900 percent viewership increase. Radio and TV news was all Michael Jackson all the time.

A veritable orgy of Jackson.

Anytime we want to question the media's, and our own, values, all we have to do is note that the combined reportage of the deaths of Anna Nicole Smith, Heath Ledger, and Michael Jackson no doubt eclipsed the amount of coverage given to all the Americans who have died in Iraq and Afghanistan.

Sad, isn't it?

Question: Does the media cover the news or make the news?

Answer: both.

***

> *The one function that TV news performs very well is that when there is no news we give it to you with the same emphasis as if there were.*
> —David Brinkley
> News Anchor

I Invented the Cell Phone

Remember how Al Gore invented the internet?

Well, I invented the cell phone.

Skeptical? Well then, just Google "Martin Cooper" and you'll see.

The Economist, in its June 6 issue, devotes two full pages to my invention. It includes a quote by one of the Federal Communications Commissioners, Robert McDowell: "Marty is the most influential person no one has ever heard of."

A back-handed compliment if ever there was one.

At first, I was incredibly proud of my invention.

It would help people seek assistance in an emergency; notify an appointment that freeway traffic would once again delay an on-time arrival; and allow children to notify parents that they were safe.

Soon every cool kid had a cell phone...they were the 21st century version of math majors walking around campus with slide rules on their belts. The *really* cool kids owned two cell phones.

And the simple concept of using my telephone without being tethered to Ma Bell's wires morphed into a little machine that could take pictures, play games, surf the Web, and of course, provide texting capabilities.

Cell phones have truly become ubiquitous. I've spotted them in the manicured palm of a woman on a treadmill at her Ventura Boulevard gym; in the gnarled hand of a horseman astride his steed in Chatsworth; and pressed against the ear of nearly everyone who crosses almost any street in our city.

Nothing is more annoying than dining in a fine restaurant and being forced to listen to someone's private cell phone conversation. Or having lunch with someone while they are texting or checking emails.

Probably the most ignored law on books is the recent ban on using cell phones while driving without the use of a hands-free device.

According to an editorial in the July 23, 2009, *New York Times*, "We find it terrifying every time we get on the highway and see all of those multitasking drivers racing along while they yammer and text on cell phones, juggle hot coffee and a Mc-whatever or attend to personal grooming in the rearview mirror."

Each year, cell phone use contributes to an estimated six percent of all crashes, which equates to 636,000 crashes, 330,000 injuries, 12,000 serious injuries and 2,600 deaths, reported the Harvard Center of Risk Analysis. They also reported that the annual cost of crashes caused by cell phone use is estimated to be $43 billion.

According to the National Safety Council, drivers who use cell phones are four times more likely to be in a crash while using a cell phone. Their research shows that "it is estimated that more than 100 million people use cell phones while driving."

What the NSC didn't report is that most of them are driving directly in front of me!

And then there's my personal favorite: people driving in the fast lane of the freeway at a leisurely 50 miles an hour while talking on their cell phones. They figure that they're safer if they drive more slowly, totally unaware of the long line of frustrated drivers behind them.

Actress Sharon Stone neatly summed up how people misuse my invention: "I drive with my knees. Otherwise, how can I put on my lipstick and talk on my phone?"

But it's hard to top the dexterity (and one might even say stupidity) of Buffalo, N.Y. area tow-truck driver Nicholas Sparks, who last month admitted to the local sheriff that he was using two cell phones at the same time while driving, one for texting and the second for talking.

He crashed his flat-bed truck through a gate and into a swimming pool...making him all wet, literally and figuratively.

Despite the recession we're grinding through, there are those who have to show that they have more than the rest of us. Even with cell phones, conspicuous consumption rears its ugly (and expensive) head.

A company called Goldstriker is selling a Nokia 8800 Arte Brilliance, which is embellished in 24-carat gold with 60 clear Swarovski crystals. It comes with a 24-

carat gold charging dock and a 24-carat gold Bluetooth accessory. It can be yours for a mere $3,275.

And because you'll want to be sure you're dealing with a reputable firm, there is a crawl across Goldstriker's website proudly proclaiming: "Goldstriker International have now opened their Flagship store at Saksaganskogo 58, Kiev, Ukraine."

Must be lots of rich – and profligate – Ukrainians.

But let's get back to the inventor of the cell phones... me.

I made the first public telephone call from a portable cell phone on April 3, 1973, while walking the streets of New York. At the time, I was the general manager of Motorola's Communications Systems Division.

Oh, I forgot to mention...there's another Marty Cooper. **He's** the one who invented the cell phone.

***

Apparently we love our own cell phones but we hate everyone else's.
—Joe Bob Briggs

Missed Opportunities...and Missed Pleasures

Sometimes you just don't know.

We all go through life sitting next to people in a meeting, working with them on a project, or encountering them at the same events...but most of the time we don't know what we don't know...and we don't know what we're missing.

Here's a good example:

I was a member of the Van Nuys Airport Citizens Advisory from 1990 to 1993, appointed by the late Councilman Marvin Braude.

At my very first meeting, when it was time for that dreaded instrument of democracy – "public comment" – I was attacked as another appointee solely interested in what was good for the business community, not the whole community.

That attack came from one of the Valley's best-known gadflies.

(There are two dictionary definitions of a "gadfly"; the first is, "a fly that irritates livestock by biting them and sucking their blood"; the second is, "somebody regarded as persistently annoying or irritating." Of course, I make reference only to the latter definition.)

By pure happenstance, at that first meeting I had seated myself next to an African-American Council member, who leaned over and said, "Don't let him upset you. He's always like that."

For the next several years, Alexton Boone and I sat next to each other, exchanging pleasantries, chatting briefly before and after the meetings. We never saw each other outside of the Council meetings.

Several years later, in July 1996, I read his obituary in the *Daily News*. The first line in Barbara Wood's obituary was: "Services have been held for Alexton Squire Boone, one of the original members of Tuskegee Airmen, the all-African-American World War II flying squadron."

There it was: Alexton Boone was a member of one of the most famous group of heroes in the war, and I never knew it.

The stories he could have told me, the people he had known, and the incredible challenges he overcame... and all I had to do was invite him to have lunch with me; it was never to be.

I was particularly vicious in verbally kicking myself since the Tuskegee Airmen had been one of my interests for years.

From 1942 through 1946, 992 Black pilots graduated from Tuskegee Army Air Field in Tuskegee, Alabama. They fought two wars: one against the Germans and another against racism from their fellow Americans.

They came out of the war with a near-unbelievable record: these fighter pilots flew 200 missions escorting bombers, and not one was lost to enemy fire. In fact, they were the Army Air Corps' (later the U.S. Air Force) only escort group that did not lose a single bomber to enemy planes.

Boone was part of a unit that destroyed or damaged 409 enemy aircraft while flying 1,578 missions, and earned a Presidential Unit Citation, 150 Distinguished Flying Crosses – more than 850 medals in all, fighting in Africa, Italy, and France.

Until 1939, the Army Air Corps refused to accept Blacks into its ranks, and it took an act of Congress to change that policy. The slights, smears, and segregation were just part of the indignities they endured...and overcame.

If you think that's a singular story, let me tell you about Ralph Tarr.

Ralph is a lawyer, one of the best (no lawyer jokes, please).

For most of the past 19 years, he has run the Los Angeles office of Andrews Kurth LLP, a Houston law firm founded in 1902. Ralph was on my executive committee when I was Chairman of VICA, and his sage but quietly delivered counsel was appreciated by all.

Unexpectedly, Andrews Kurth shuttered their Los Angeles office, another recession victim. When I heard about it, I asked Ralph to give me a copy of his resumé so I could share it with others I know in his field.

Now I've seen lots of impressive resumés before, but not many could match Ralph's. But what really caught my eye was the fact that he was the chief legal counsel for the U.S. Department of the Interior...and he chaired the entire investigation and legal issues surrounding the Exxon Valdez Alaskan oil spill.

...And just months ago I had completed a lengthy chapter on crisis management that will soon be published in a book on that topic. Of course, I spent hours and hours researching the crisis communications issues related to...the Exxon Valdez oil spill.

Had I but known that this was just one of Ralph Tarr's arrows in his legal quiver I could have saved weeks of work, and gotten the facts directly from – as it were – the horse's mouth.

Previously, Ralph was the U.S. Attorney General's lawyer, and has held lots of other impressive positions in the federal and state governments and as a successful law firm partner...but I missed out on getting the inside scoop on the Exxon Valdez story.

Sometimes you just don't know.

**

There is no shame in not knowing; the shame lies in not finding out.
—Russian proverb

Showing Their Mettle with a Medal

So, David Honda won the Fernando Award and Barack Obama received the Nobel Peace Prize.

We humans love to win awards, medals, commendations, or whatever one calls that which separates us from the herd.

In show biz, the Oscars, Emmys, Tonys, and a few dozen more of diminishing importance, are more than recognition, they are often worth millions in the bank.

Of course, there are those who put their distinctions in the proper perspective: Speaking to the 300th graduating class of his alma mater, Yale University, on May 21, 2001, President George W. Bush said, "To those of you who received honors, awards and distinctions, may I say, well done." And then, with a wry grin, he added, "and to the C students, I say, you too can be President of the United States."

Our military, like those of almost every nation, bestows medals and ribbons upon those who have sacrificed in time of war. Our highest recognition is simply called the "Medal of Honor." Since it is presented by the President on behalf of the Congress, it is usually – although inaccurately – called the "Congressional Medal of Honor."

Nearly 150 years ago, on December 9, 1861, Senator James W. Grimes of Iowa introduced a bill calling for the production and distribution of "medals of honor". President Lincoln signed the bill and the Medal of Honor was born.

While there is nothing in the Uniform Code of Military Justice that mandates that a Medal of Honor recipient be saluted by a general, admiral, or any other officer – including the Commander in Chief – it is a long-standing informal tradition that is nearly universally adhered to in the armed services.

It is not the man (there are no living women Medal of Honor recipients) who is being saluted, it is the award.

There have been a total of 3,448 honorees, 95 of whom are still living. Nineteen individuals have won this award twice.

The only woman awarded the Medal of Honor, Mary Walker, was recognized for her bravery at the Battle of Bull Run on July 21, 1861.

There have been 87 African-American, 41 Hispanic-American, 31 Asian-American, and 22 Native-American recipients of the Medal of Honor.

These are some of my favorite-named awards from other countries: Mongolian Order of the Polar Star (USSR), Anti-Partisan Badge (Nazi Germany), Healthcare Reservist of the Year (Wales), Order of the Bath (United Kingdom), Order of Saint Andrew the First-Called (Imperial Russia), Order of the White Eagle (Poland), Medal of Brilliant Helmet (Taiwan), Golden Leopard Award (South Africa), Order of Michael the

Brave (Romania), Order of the Golden Fleece (Spain), and the Order of Bogdan Khmelnitsky (Ukraine).

Here in Our Valley, we're equally dedicated to awards.

Here are some popular Valley recognitions; can you match them with the organizations that bestow them?

The awards: 1) The Golden Horn, 2) Circle of Life, 3) Steve Allen Excellence in Education Award, 4) Joseph Staller Award, and 5) Ken Banks Award.

The organizations: a) Valley Economic Alliance, b) Valley Cultural Center, c) Woodland Hills-Tarzana Chamber, d) Universal City North Hollywood Chamber, e) Jewish Home for the Aging's Executives (answers below).

Most awards given out by Valley organizations are to recognize – and therefore stimulate – volunteerism or community service.

I have always believed that there is a co-mingling of honors that should be separated.

Individuals who are tasked to become involved in supporting communities as part of their job should not be included in the same awards category as those who volunteer and assist charitable organizations and social agencies on their own.

Similarly, those who are active in chambers of commerce and other business organizations should not be recognized in the same category as those who support the Pacific Lodge Boys Home, Haven Hills, New Horizons, or New Directions for Youth.

Therefore, I propose a new, three-award approach to recognition:

- The Medal of Mulholland Curve with Oak Leaf Clusters is to be awarded to the best performance in community service by someone who is paid to do so. Serving as an officer in any civic, philanthropic, or community organization shall entitle such a medal winner to a five percent salary bonus.

- The Order of Leonis Adobe Stucco with Crossed Trowels shall be bestowed upon an individual who has contributed significantly to Valley business and civic organizations. Special recognition is to be given to an awardee who has attended more than 25 mixers in any one year.

- The Edgar Rice Burroughs Honorific with Jane and Cheetah Rampant is to be pinned to the chest of someone who has excelled in true volunteerism with charitable organizations or social agencies with no thought of personal gain. Those who are recognized with this award must, prior to receiving the Honorific, attest to have never monkeyed around.

Answers: Golden Horn (b), Circle of Life (e), Steve Allen Excellence in Education Award (a), Joseph Staller Award (c), Ken Banks Award (d).

***

> *I don't deserve this award, but I have arthritis and I don't deserve that either.*
> —Jack Benny

What's the Valley's Next Big Thing?

We humans are always in search of The Next Big Thing.

I remember a cartoon in *Playboy Magazine* (I only read it for the cartoons) with two cavemen talking to each other. One was holding a primitive bow and arrow and boastfully said to his friend, "I think I've developed the ultimate weapon."

Back in the late 1940s, we were sure we had created not only The Next Big Thing, but The Ultimate Weapon, in the atomic bomb.

Then The Next Big Thing in weapons was the hydrogen bomb. Ronald Reagan's near-fanciful array of weapons in space, Star Wars, was intended to be the ultimate Big Thing.

Today?

In a nod to lethal retro, the most effective weapon used against our soldiers in Iraq and Afghanistan is something called an Improvised Explosive Device (IED), made with, according to a recent interview with an on-the-ground American soldier there, $10 worth of materials.

And then there's The Next Big Thing in technology.

Last week I heard from one of my younger technosavvy friends that email is now obsolete...just when I've mastered it. Today's Next Big Things are Facebook, Twitter, LinkedIn, and other quasi-cleverly-named applications.

But the coming of the computer and Internet technology were not always seen as The Next Big Thing.

In 1943, Thomas Watson, chairman of IBM, said, "I think there is a world market for maybe five computers."

As recently as 1977, Ken Olson, the president, chairman, and founder of Digital Equipment Corp., prophesied, "There is no reason anyone would want a computer in their home."

Other technical inventions were greeted with no more respect.

Broadcast pioneer David Sarnoff urged an investment in radio back in the 1920s. One of his associates responded with a memo: "The wireless music box has no imaginable commercial value. Who would pay for a message sent to nobody in particular?"

Equally prescient (not) was the Western Union executive who authored this 1876 internal memo: "This 'telephone' has too many shortcomings to be seriously considered as a means of communication. The device is inherently of no value to us."

But The Next Big Thing isn't only mechanical or technical; it can be people.

Remember when, just a few years ago, The Next Big Thing in Los Angeles was (drum roll, please) Antonio

Villaraigosa. Latino mayor of the second-biggest city in the nation. Cover boy on *Time* and *Newsweek* magazines. Shoo-in as Arnold's replacement.

No longer.

Familiarity may not necessarily breed contempt, but it does breed familiarity.

The Next Big Thing today in City Hall (actually, across the street in the new yet-to-be-named police headquarters) is our new LAPD Chief, Charlie Beck.

In our nation's business development, the first Next Big Thing was probably Henry Ford and the assembly line. Since then, creativity, technology, and capitalistic drive led to The American Corporation, a sometimes-dehumanizing but highly profitable and exceedingly efficient approach to manufacturing, distribution, and marketing.

They made it and we came...and bought.

In Our Valley, we've had some Next Big Things.

Lockheed's Skunk Works, now the site of Bob Hope Airport, produced some great Next Big Things in the history of aviation, particularly World War II aircraft. Some of the greatest advances in space travel engines came from Rocketdyne, just up the road apiece in Canoga Park.

But the Biggest Big Thing to come out of the Valley was the motion picture industry, thanks to a German Jewish immigrant, Carl Laemmle, who took 230 acres and built the world's largest film studio in 1915, where it still resides today, overlooking the Cahuenga Pass.

So what's The Next Big Thing in Our Valley's business growth?

It's the same Big Thing we've been focusing on for decades: entrepreneurialism.

As America looks with disgust at overblown corporate compensation packages, winces at Wall Street's ability to generate millions through arcane financial instruments, and recoils from large industry groups gaming the system in Sacramento and Washington, D.C., the entrepreneur continues to do his (and her) thing.

The Valley is awash with people opening restaurants, banks, and retail stores; making technological advances; devising medical equipment; starting firms focusing on all things "green."

Many of these will fall by the wayside, but many will survive and thrive. They will grow, provide jobs, support the community, and fuel our future growth.

Our Valley has a major university and numerous colleges sending forth into the workplace minds that will innovate, create, and build.

What's The Next Big Thing? We are.

***

Heavier-than-air flying machines are impossible.

– Lord Kelvin
President, 1885
The Royal Society

Cause-Related Marketing Good for the Bottom Line

When it's played right, giving can beget getting...and this is the season for it.

Straight-out philanthropy, or donations for no material return, is the most welcome kind of support for cash-strapped non-profits. But gathering steam over the past half-century has been the concept of cause-related marketing.

Using support of, and involvement with, non-profit organizations and social agencies for mutual benefit goes back a long time, but its modern application is just decades old.

One of the earliest such national campaigns was 7-Eleven's Save a Living Thing Campaign, back in the '70s. 7-Eleven wanted to increase sales of its Slurpee (was there ever a better-named drink?) product, and the concept of environmentalism was just gaining primacy.

The promotion was simple: customers would go into a 7-Eleven and purchase a Slurpee with a bald eagle, a cougar, or another endangered species printed on the outside of the cup; you'd use the cup with the artwork corresponding to the species you wanted to help save. For every cup, a nickel would go to the non-profit organization focusing on helping save that particular species.

7-Eleven obtained reams of positive media coverage and tens of thousands of dollars went to the World Wildlife Fund and similar organizations.

American Express is credited with conceiving the term "cause-related marketing," using that phrase to describe activities that support local charitable causes while promoting business at the same time. Its most successful incarnation was the marketing campaign American Express embarked on to restore the Statue of Liberty in 1983.

Each time cardholders would use their card, a penny was donated to the Statue of Liberty renovation campaign. For every new card account opened, the company donated a dollar to the campaign. Over just four months, $2 million was raised; American Express card usage jumped by an incredible 28 percent!

According to a 2006 research project, the Cone Millennial Cause Study, 89 percent of Americans would switch from one brand to another of comparable price and quality if the latter brand was associated with a "good cause."

And just in case you think cause marketing is only for the big, national companies, consider Ben Forat, who owns Studio City Car Wash.

Ben's PR consultant, Jack McGrath, recommended that he look into cause-related marketing program, partially as an antidote to a sign dispute with the City, partially because it's good business.

They selected a local school, Colfax Avenue Elementary, and created a program to benefit both the car wash and the school. The school's students distribute cards to retailers throughout the area (dry cleaners, restaurants, liquor stores, etc.) that promote using Studio City Car Wash on Sundays, pointing out that by presenting the card, the car wash will make a contribution to the school for the full amount of the wash – $12.

So while the car wash doesn't make any money on the Sunday wash, just imagine the community support, positive PR value, and future business, it receives from the program.

The program has been so successful that it's been expanded to other local schools.

Simi Valley Ford is another example of a local organization helping raise money for local schools by inviting customers to visit their dealership and test drive a new Ford on a certain date. For every test drive completed, Ford donated $20, up to $6,000 total, to Royal and Simi Valley High Schools in support of special programs.

But is that type of support given to other for-profit organizations and local non-profits?

For example, among the national sponsors of the Boys & Girls Clubs of America are such blue-chip names as Coca-Cola, Taco Bell, JCPenney, Major League Baseball Charities, Staples, Microsoft, Staples, AT&T, UPS, Wal-Mart, and Bank of America.

Wouldn't it be interesting to know how those national brands translate that support to programs here in Our

Valley? Not just annual donations, but actual joint marketing programs that would benefit both the Clubs and the corporate entities.

One national sponsor has indeed supported a Valley-based organization.

In April, August, and October, Northridge JCPenney customers were invited to "round up" their purchases to the nearest dollar. As a result, just a few weeks ago, $5,226 was donated by JCPenney to the Boys & Girls Club of the West Valley for its after-school programs.

Good for JCPenney; good for the Boys & Girls Club.

Habitat for Humanity's website lists more than 40 corporate partners, including: Bank of America, Coldwell Banker, Delta Air Lines, Home Depot, Lowe's, the National Basketball Association, the National Hockey League, Nissan, PG&E, State Farm Insurance, Subaru, and many more.

According to Donna Deutchman, CEO of this region's Habitat for Humanity affiliate, when Lowe's in Pacoima held its Grand Opening on June 18, they promoted their Buy a Gift Card, Help Build a Home program. Anyone who purchased a Lowe's Gift Card that day had their purchase matched by Lowe's, up to $5,000, to support the next Habitat building project.

Perhaps we need a focus on the creativity that inspires businesses here in the Valley figure out how they can help themselves while helping the community.

Besides, isn't December the right time for Santa Cause-related marketing?

***

> *My father used to say, "You can spend a lot of time making money. The tough time comes when you have to give it away properly." How to give something back, that's the tough part in life.*
> —Lee Iacocca

AT&T's Sales Scam: They're Phoning It In

In my youth (parts of which I can still dimly remember), I wanted to be a crusading reporter or a muckraker like Lincoln Steffens, Ida Tarbell, or Upton Sinclair.

Latter-day muckrakers, such as Bob Woodward and Carl Bernstein (can you think of one without the other?) and Ralph Nader, held little appeal to me.

Over the nearly five years, Ye Olde Editor of the *Business Journal* has suffered the vagaries of this column in resigned acquiescence, we have taken a shot or two at such easy targets as Angelo Mozilo, the *Los Angeles Times*, and numerous City Hall denizens.

So here's one more: the latest scam perpetrated on us by what used to be known as Ma Bell, with all the warmth and caring such a nickname once connoted.

First of all, AT&T isn't really the Bell System or American Telephone & Telegraph anymore. It's the product of deregulation and divestitures; mergers and mandates; and spinoffs and stock swaps.

And for those of us who care about American history, business ingenuity, and ability to adapt to technological advances, AT&T's descent into its present deceitful business practices is a sad one. For example:

Recently, my associate Terry Stevens received a call from someone "calling on behalf of AT&T," informing her that Cooper Communications' current telephone plan was not the best one for us. As a result, Terry changed to the recommended plan.

End of story, right?

Wrong...

Since that time, we have received at least ten more calls from AT&T asking us to switch to another plan. Each time, Terry informed the AT&T representative that we had already switched, and asked to have us removed from their call list.

Each time, they assured her it would be done.

By the fourth call, she asked to speak to a supervisor. Apparently, however, calling representatives are instructed not to make a supervisor available, because she never did get one on the phone; each time the call would mysteriously be disconnected or she would be put into the maddening voice-prompt system to rot for eternity.

As it turns out, the aggressive phone calls were just the start of the problem. When we received the bill with the upgraded plan, our cost was not reduced at all; it was $80 higher than our previous bill!

Irritated, Terry called AT&T directly to discuss the bill and the ongoing calls. Enter James...

James explained that the unsolicited calls we had been receiving were not from AT&T employees at all, but from independent solicitors who are paid by AT&T on a commission-only basis to sell you an upgraded plan.

He admitted that he receives calls "all day long" from angry customers who have upgraded to unnecessary plans on the advice of commission-only AT&T solicitors assuming the threadbare mantle of a helpful customer service rep.

James also explained that the plan we had been sold was "way more than we needed" based upon his review; he put us back on our original plan.

That done, Terry asked why we continued to be targeted even though she'd made numerous requests to be removed from the commissioned solicitors' call lists.

The answer, of course, is that since these solicitors are not paid to do anything but to switch customers to a more expensive plan, they certainly are not going to waste time taking us off their call list. If you want to get off AT&T's call list, you have to call the company, not depend on a call you receive from a salesperson.

On December 10, I received a call from "Robert," who identified himself as an "AT&T account specialist," from "Las Vegas, you know, the City of Light."

I always thought Paris was the City of Light, but what do I know?

And then finally, a call came in from Edward Parker, calling, he said, from Orlando, Florida; he even gave me his AT&T company ID, #9205EP. He offered to fax information showing that the plan he was offering was more cost-effective than the one we had...We're still waiting for that fax.

And of course, there is no AT&T employee named Edward Parker, and that's not an AT&T employee number.

I know this will come as a huge shock to *Business Journal* readers, but phone service plans are *designed* to be confusing. Between the various plans, upgrades, extras, special offers, and everything else they throw at you, it's impossible to keep up with what's best for your business. Best bet: call AT&T periodically and have them review your bill to make sure your current plan is the best one for you.

Oh, yes, on top of everything else, it appears that "upgrade" prices are subjective, based on who's selling it to you. After Terry signed up for the $51 long distance plan, she received a call several days later telling her she could upgrade to that same plan... for $60 a month!

To make matters worse, if you *do* change your plan, there are penalty fees associated with early withdrawal.

When Terry spoke with James, she asked to be put on a "no solicitation" list. He told her he would do so but that it might take up to 30 days. Since that time we have received at least three more calls, with another week to go before the 30-day mark....we shall see.

Is there any irony in the fact that "Alexander Graham Bell" rhymes with "Telephone Hell"?

***

I would throw my phone away if I could get away with it.
— Tom Hanks

LaVergne, TN USA
18 August 2010
193822LV00003B/4/P